Edith van Dyne

Aunt Jane's Nieces on the Ranch

Edith van Dyne

Aunt Jane's Nieces on the Ranch

1st Edition | ISBN: 978-3-75232-774-8

Place of Publication: Frankfurt am Main, Germany

Year of Publication: 2020

Outlook Verlag GmbH, Germany.

Aunt Jane's Nieces on the Ranch
By
EDITH VAN DYNE

CHAPTER I—UNCLE JOHN DECIDES

"And now," said Major Doyle, rubbing his hands together as he half reclined in his big chair in a corner of the sitting room, "now we shall enjoy a nice cosy winter in dear New York."

"Cosy?" said his young daughter, Miss Patricia Doyle, raising her head from her sewing to cast a glance through the window at the whirling snowflakes.

"Ab-so-lute-ly cosy, Patsy, my dear," responded the major. "Here we are in our own steam-heated flat—seven rooms and a bath, not counting the closets—hot water any time you turn the faucet; a telephone call brings the butcher, the baker, the candlestick-maker; latest editions of the papers chucked into the passage! What more do you want?"

"Tcha!"

This scornful ejaculation came from a little bald-headed man seated in the opposite corner, who had been calmly smoking his pipe and dreamily eyeing the flickering gas-log in the grate. The major gave a start and turned to stare fixedly at the little man. Patsy, scenting mischief, indulged in a little laugh as she threaded her needle.

"Sir! what am I to understand from that brutal interruption?" demanded Major Doyle sternly.

"You're talking nonsense," was the reply, uttered in a tone of cheery indifference. "New York in winter is a nightmare. Blizzards, thaws, hurricanes, ice, la grippe, shivers—grouches."

"Drumsticks!" cried the major indignantly. "It's the finest climate in the world—bar none. We've the finest restaurants, the best theatres, the biggest stores and—and the stock exchange. And then, there's Broadway! What more can mortal desire, John Merrick?"

The little man laughed, but filled his pipe without reply.

"Uncle John is getting uneasy," observed Patsy. "I've noticed it for some time. This is the first snowstorm that has caught him in New York for several years."

"The blizzard came unusually early," said Mr. Merrick apologetically. "It took me by surprise. But I imagine there will be a few days more of decent weather before winter finally sets in. By that time—"

"Well, what then?" asked the major in defiant accents, as his brother-in-law hesitated.

"By that time we shall be out of it, of course," was the quiet reply.

Patsy looked at her uncle reflectively, while the major grunted and shifted uneasily in his chair. Father and daughter were alike devoted to John Merrick, whose generosity and kindliness had rescued them from poverty and thrust upon them all the comforts they now enjoyed. Even this pretty flat building in Willing Square, close to the fashionable New York residence district, belonged in fee to Miss Doyle, it having been a gift from her wealthy uncle. And Uncle John made his home with them, quite content in a seven-room-flat when his millions might have purchased the handsomest establishment in the metropolis. Down in Wall Street and throughout the financial districts the name of the great John Merrick was mentioned with awe; here in Willing Square he smoked a pipe in his corner of the modest sitting room and cheerfully argued with his irascible brother-in-law, Major Doyle, whose business it was to look after Mr. Merrick's investments and so allow the democratic little millionaire the opportunity to come and go as he pleased.

The major's greatest objection to Uncle John's frequent absences from New York—especially during the winter months—was due to the fact that his beloved Patsy, whom he worshiped with a species of idolatry, usually accompanied her uncle. It was quite natural for the major to resent being left alone, and equally natural for Patsy to enjoy these travel experiences, which in Uncle John's company were always delightful.

Patsy Doyle was an unprepossessing little thing, at first sight. She was short of stature and a bit plump; freckled and red-haired; neat and wholesome in appearance but lacking "style" in either form or apparel. But to her friends Patricia was beautiful. Her big blue eyes, mischievous and laughing, won hearts without effort, and the girl was so genuine—so natural and unaffected —that she attracted old and young alike and boasted a host of admiring friends.

This girl was Uncle John's favorite niece, but not the only one. Beth De Graf, a year younger than her cousin Patsy, was a ward of Mr. Merrick and lived with the others in the little flat at Willing Square. Beth was not an orphan, but her father and mother, residents of an Ohio town, had treated the girl so selfishly and inconsiderately that she had passed a very unhappy life until Uncle John took her under his wing and removed Beth from her depressing environment. This niece was as beautiful in form and feature as Patsy Doyle was plain, but she did not possess Patsy's cheerful and uniform temperament and was by nature reserved and diffident in the presence of strangers.

Yet Beth had many good qualities, among them a heart-felt sympathy for young girls who were not so fortunate as herself. On this disagreeable winter's day she had set out to visit a settlement school where she had long since proved herself the good angel of a score of struggling girls. The blizzard had developed since she left home, but no one worried about her, for Beth was very resourceful.

There was another niece, likewise dear to John Merrick's heart, who had been Louise Merrick before she married a youth named Arthur Weldon, some two years before this story begins. A few months ago Arthur had taken his young wife to California, where he had purchased a fruit ranch, and there a baby was born to them which they named "Jane Merrick Weldon"—a rather big name for what was admitted to be a very small person.

This baby, now five months old and reported to be thriving, had been from its birth of tremendous interest to every inhabitant of the Willing Square flat. It had been discussed morning, noon and night by Uncle John and the girls, while even the grizzled major was not ashamed to admit that "that Weldon infant" was an important addition to the family. Perhaps little Jane acquired an added interest by being so far away from all her relatives, as well as from the fact that Louise wrote such glowing accounts of the baby's beauty and witcheries that to believe a tithe of what she asserted was to establish the child as an infantile marvel.

Now, Patsy Doyle knew in her heart that Uncle John was eager to see Louise's baby, and long ago she had confided to Beth her belief that the winter would find Mr. Merrick at Arthur Weldon's California ranch, with all his three nieces gathered around him and the infantile marvel in his arms. The same suspicion had crept into Major Doyle's mind, and that is why he so promptly resented the suggestion that New York was not an ideal winter resort. Somehow, the old major "felt in his bones" that his beloved Patsy would be whisked away to California, leaving her father to face the tedious winter without her; for he believed his business duties would not allow him to get away to accompany her.

Yet so far Uncle John, in planning for the winter, had not mentioned California as even a remote possibility. It was understood he would go somewhere, but up to the moment when he declared "we will be out of it, of course, when the bad weather sets in," he had kept his own counsel and forborne to express a preference or a decision.

But now the major, being aroused, decided to "have it out" with his elusive brother-in-law.

"Where will ye go to find a better place?" he demanded.

"We're going to Bermuda," said Uncle John.

"For onions?" asked the major sarcastically.

"They have other things in Bermuda besides onions. A delightful climate, I'm told, is one of them."

The major sniffed. He was surprised, it is true, and rather pleased, because Bermuda is so much nearer New York than is California; but it was his custom to object.

"Patsy can't go," he declared, as if that settled the question for good and all. "The sea voyage would kill her. I'm told by truthful persons that the voyage to Bermuda is the most terrible experience known to mortals. Those who don't die on the way over positively refuse ever to come back again, and so remain forever exiled from their homes and families—until they have the good luck to die from continually eating onions."

Mr. Merrick smiled as he glanced at the major's severe countenance.

"It can't be as bad as that," said he. "I know a man who has taken his family to Bermuda for five winters, in succession."

"And brought 'em back alive each time?"

"Certainly. Otherwise, you will admit he couldn't take them again."

"That family," asserted the major seriously, "must be made of cast-iron, with clockwork stomachs."

Patsy gave one of her low, musical laughs.

"I think I would like Bermuda," she said. "Anyhow, whatever pleases Uncle John will please me, so long as we get away from New York."

"Why, ye female traitor!" cried the major; and added, for Uncle John's benefit: "New York is admitted by men of discretion to be the modern Garden of Eden. It's the one desideratum of—"

Here the door opened abruptly and Beth came in. Her cheeks were glowing red from contact with the wind and her dark tailor-suit glistened with tiny drops left by the melted snow. In her mittened hand she waved a letter.

"From Louise, Patsy!" she exclaimed, tossing it toward her cousin; "but don't you dare read it till I've changed my things."

Then she disappeared into an inner room and Patsy, disregarding the injunction, caught up the epistle and tore open the envelope.

Uncle John refilled his pipe and looked at Patsy's tense face inquiringly. The major stiffened, but could not wholly repress his curiosity. After a moment he said:

"All well, Patsy?"

"How's the baby?" asked Uncle John.

"Dear me!" cried Patsy, with a distressed face; "and no doctor nearer than five miles!"

Both men leaped from their chairs.

"Why don't they keep a doctor in the house?" roared the major.

"Suppose we send Dr. Lawson, right away!" suggested Uncle John.

Patsy, still holding up the letter, turned her eyes upon them reproachfully.

"It's all over," she said with a sigh.

The major dropped into a chair, limp and inert. Uncle John paled.

"The—the baby isn't—dead!" he gasped.

"No, indeed," returned Patsy, again reading. "But it had colic most dreadfully, and Louise was in despair. But the nurse, a dark-skinned Mexican creature, gave it a dose of some horrid hot stuff—"

"Chile con carne, most likely!" ejaculated the major.

"Horrible!" cried Uncle John.

"And that cured the colic but almost burned poor little Jane's insides out."

"Insides out!"

"However, Louise says the dear baby is now quite well again," continued the girl.

"Perhaps so, when she wrote," commented the major, wiping his forehead with a handkerchief; "but that's a week ago, at least. A thousand things might have happened to that child since then. Why was Arthur Weldon such a fool as to settle in a desert place, far away from all civilization? He ought to be prosecuted for cruelty."

"The baby's all right," said Patsy, soothingly. "If anything serious happened, Louise would telegraph."

"I doubt it," said the major, walking the floor. "I doubt if there's such a thing as a telegraph in all that forsaken country."

Uncle John frowned.

"You are getting imbecile, Major. They've a lot more comforts and conveniences on that ranch than we have here in New York."

"Name 'em!" shouted the Major. "I challenge ye to mention one thing we haven't right here in this flat."

"Chickens!" said Beth, re-entering the room in time to hear this challenge. "How's the baby, Patsy?"

"Growing like a weed, dear, and getting more lovely and cunning every second. Here—read the letter yourself."

While Beth devoured the news from California Uncle John replied to the major.

"At El Cajon Ranch," said he, "there's a fine big house where the sunshine peeps in and floods the rooms every day in the year. Hear that blizzard howl outside, and think of the roses blooming this instant on the trellis of Louise's window. Arthur has two automobiles and can get to town in twenty minutes. They've a long-distance telephone and I've talked with 'em over the line several times."

"You have!" This in a surprised chorus.

"I have. Only last week I called Louise up."

"An expensive amusement, John," said the major grimly.

"Yes; but I figured I could afford it. I own some telephone stock, you know, so I may get part of that investment back. They have their own cows, and chickens—as Beth truly says—and any morning they can pick oranges and grapefruit from their own trees for breakfast."

"I'd like to see that precious baby," remarked Beth, laying the letter on her lap to glance pleadingly at her uncle.

"Uncle John is going to take us to Bermuda," said Patsy in a serious voice.

The little man flushed and sat down abruptly. The major, noting his attitude, became disturbed.

"You've all made the California trip," said he. "It doesn't pay to see any country twice."

"But we haven't seen Arthur's ranch," Beth reminded him.

"Nor the baby," added Patsy, regarding the back of Uncle John's head somewhat wistfully.

The silence that followed was broken only by the major's low growls. The poor man already knew his fate.

"That chile-con-carne nurse ought to be discharged," mumbled Uncle John, half audibly. "Mexicans are stupid creatures to have around. I think we ought to take with us an experienced nurse, who is intelligent and up-to-date."

"Oh, I know the very one!" exclaimed Beth. "Mildred Travers. She's perfectly splendid. I've watched her with that poor girl who was hurt at the school, and she's as gentle and skillful as she is refined. Mildred would bring up that baby to be as hearty and healthful as a young savage."

"How soon could she go?" asked Uncle John.

"At an hour's notice, I'm sure. Trained nurses are used to sudden calls, you know. I'll see her to-morrow—if it's better weather."

"Do," said Uncle John. "I suppose you girls can get ready by Saturday?"

"Of course!" cried Patsy and Beth in one voice.

"Then I'll make the reservations. Major Doyle, you will arrange your business to accompany us."

"I won't!"

"You will, or I'll discharge you. You're working for me, aren't you?"

"I am, sir."

"Then obey orders."

CHAPTER II—EL CAJON RANCH

Uncle John always traveled comfortably and even luxuriously, but without ostentation. Such conveniences as were offered the general public he indulged in, but no one would suspect him of being a multi-millionaire who might have ordered a special train of private cars had the inclination seized him. A modest little man, who had made an enormous fortune in the far Northwest— almost before he realized it—John Merrick had never allowed the possession of money to deprive him of his simple tastes or to alter his kindly nature. He loved to be of the people and to mingle with his fellows on an equal footing, and nothing distressed him more than to be recognized by some one as the great New York financier. It is true that he had practically retired from business, but his huge fortune was invested in so many channels that his name remained prominent among men of affairs and this notoriety he was unable wholly to escape.

The trip to California was a delight because none of his fellow passengers knew his identity. During the three days' jaunt from Chicago to Los Angeles he was recognized only as an engaging little man who was conducting a party of three charming girls, as well as a sedate, soldierly old gentleman, into the sunny Southland for a winter's recreation.

Of these three girls we already know Patsy Doyle and Beth DeGraf, but Mildred Travers remains to be introduced. The trained nurse whom Beth had secured was tall and slight, with a sweet face, a gentle expression and eyes so calm and deep that a stranger found it disconcerting to gaze within them. Beth herself had similar eyes—big and fathomless—yet they were so expressive as to allure and bewitch the beholder, while Mildred Travers' eyes repelled one as being masked—as concealing some well guarded secret. Both the major and Uncle John had felt this and it made the latter somewhat uneasy when he reflected that he was taking this girl to be the trusted nurse of Louise's precious baby. He questioned Beth closely concerning Mildred and his niece declared that no kindlier, more sympathetic or more skillful nurse was ever granted a diploma. Of Mildred's history she was ignorant, except that the girl had confided to her the story of her struggles to obtain recognition and to get remunerative work after graduating from the training school.

"Once, you know," explained Beth, "trained nurses were in such demand that none were ever idle; but the training schools have been turning them out in such vast numbers that only those with family influence are now sure of work. Mildred is by instinct helpful and sympathetic—a natural born nurse, Uncle John—but because she was practically a stranger in New York she was forced to do charity and hospital work, and that is how I became acquainted with her."

"She seems to bear out your endorsement, except for her eyes," said Uncle John. "I—I don't like—her eyes. They're hard. At times they seem vengeful and cruel, like tigers' eyes."

"Oh, you wrong Mildred, I'm sure!" exclaimed Beth, and Uncle John reluctantly accepted her verdict. On the journey Miss Travers appeared well bred and cultured, conversing easily and intelligently on a variety of subjects, yet always exhibiting a reserve, as if she held herself to be one apart from the others. Indeed, the girl proved so agreeable a companion that Mr. Merrick's misgivings gradually subsided. Even the major, still suspicious and doubtful, admitted that Mildred was "quite a superior person."

Louise had been notified by telegraph of the coming of her relatives, but they had withheld from her the fact that they were bringing a "proper" nurse to care for the Weldon baby. The party rested a day in Los Angeles and then journeyed on to Escondido, near which town the Weldon ranch was located.

Louise and Arthur were both at the station with their big seven-passenger touring car. The young mother was promptly smothered in embraces by Patsy and Beth, but when she emerged from this ordeal to be hugged and kissed by Uncle John, that observing little gentleman decided that she looked exactly as girlish and lovely as on her wedding day.

This eldest niece was, in fact, only twenty years of age—quite too young to be a wife and mother. She was of that feminine type which matures slowly and seems to bear the mark of perpetual youth. Mrs. Weldon's slight, willowy form was still almost childlike in its lines, and the sunny, happy smile upon her face seemed that of a school-maid.

That tall, boyish figure beside her, now heartily welcoming the guests, would scarcely be recognized as belonging to a husband and father. These two were more like children playing at "keeping house" than sedate married people. Mildred Travers observed the couple with evident surprise; but the others, familiar with the love story of Arthur and Louise, were merely glad to find them unchanged and enjoying their former health and good spirits.

"The baby!"

That was naturally the first inquiry, voiced in concert by the late arrivals; and Louise, blushing prettily and with a delightful air of proprietorship, laughingly assured them that "Toodlums" was very well.

"This is such a glorious country," she added as the big car started off with its load, to be followed by a wagon with the baggage, "that every living thing flourishes here like the green bay trees—and baby is no exception. Oh, you'll love our quaint old home, Uncle John! And, Patsy, we've got such a flock of white chickens! And there's a new baby calf, Beth! And the major shall sleep in the Haunted Room, and—"

"Haunted?" asked the major, his eyes twinkling.

"I'm sure they're rats," said the little wife, "but the Mexicans claim it's the old miser himself. And the oranges are just in their prime and the roses are simply magnificent!"

So she rambled on, enthusiastic over her ranch home one moment and the next asking eager questions about New York and her old friends there. Louise had a mother, who was just now living in Paris, much to Arthur

Weldon's satisfaction. Even Louise did not miss the worldly-minded, self-centered mother with whom she had so little in common, and perhaps Uncle John and his nieces would never have ventured on this visit had Mrs. Merrick been at the ranch.

The California country roads are all "boulevards," although they are nothing more than native earth, rolled smooth and saturated with heavy oil until they resemble asphalt. The automobile was a fast one and it swept through the beautiful country, all fresh and green in spite of the fact that it was December, and fragrant with the scent of roses and carnations, which bloomed on every side, until a twenty-minute run brought them to an avenue of gigantic palms which led from the road up to the ranch house of El Cajon.

Originally El Cajon had been a Spanish grant of several thousand acres, and three generations of Spanish dons had resided there. The last of these Cristovals had erected the present mansion—a splendid, rambling dwelling built around an open court where a fountain splashed and tall palms shot their swaying crowns far above the housetop. The South Wing was the old dwelling which the builder had incorporated into the present scheme, but the newer part was the more imposing.

The walls were of great thickness and composed of adobe blocks of huge size. These were not sun-baked, as is usual in adobe dwellings, but had been burned like brick in a furnace constructed for the purpose by the first proprietor, and were therefore much stronger and harder than ordinary brick. In this climate there is no dampness clinging to such a structure and the rooms were extraordinarily cool in summer and warm in the chill winter season. Surrounding the house were many magnificent trees of tropical and semi-tropical nature, all of which had now attained their full prime. On the south and east sides were extensive rose gardens and beds of flowers in wonderful variety.

It was here that the last Señor Cristoval had brought his young bride, a lady of Madrid who was reputed to have possessed great beauty; but seclusion in this retired spot, then much isolated, rendered her so unhappy that she became mentally unbalanced and in a fit of depression took her own life. Cristoval, until then a generous and noble man, was completely changed by this catastrophe. During the remainder of his life he was noted for parsimony and greed for money, not unmixed with cruelty. He worked his ignorant Indian and Mexican servants mercilessly, denying them proper food or wage, and his death was a relief to all. Afterward the big estate was cut up and passed into various hands. Three hundred acres of fine orange and olive groves, including the spacious mansion, were finally sold to young Arthur Weldon.

"It's an awfully big place," said Louise, as the party alighted and stood upon the broad stone veranda, "but it is so quaint and charming that I love every stick and stone of it."

"The baby!" shrieked Patsy.

"Where's that blessed baby?" cried Beth.

Then came from the house a dusky maid bearing in her arms a soft, fluffy bundle that was instantly pounced upon by the two girls, to Uncle John's horror and dismay.

"Be careful, there!" he called. "You'll smother the poor thing." But Louise laughed and regarded the scene delightedly. And little Jane seemed to appreciate the importance of the occasion, for she waved her tiny hands and cooed a welcome to her two new aunties.

CHAPTER III—THAT BLESSED BABY!

"Oh, you darling!"

"It's my turn, Patsy! Don't be selfish. Let me kiss her again."

"That's enough, Beth. Here—give me my niece!"

"She's mine, too."

"Give me that baby! There; you've made her cry."

"I haven't; she's laughing because I kissed her wee nose."

"Isn't she a dear, though?"

"Now, girls," suggested Louise, "suppose we give Uncle John and the major a peep at her."

Reluctantly the bundle was abandoned to its mother, who carried it to where Mr. Merrick was nervously standing. "Yes, yes," he said, touching one cheek gently with the tip of his finger. "It—it's a fine child, Louise; really a—a—creditable child. But—eh—isn't it rather—soft?"

"Of course, Uncle John. All babies are soft. Aren't you going to kiss little Jane?"

"It—won't—hurt it?"

"Not a bit. Haven't Beth and Patsy nearly kissed its skin off?"

"Babies," asserted Major Doyle, stiffly, "were made to be kissed. Anyhow, that's the penalty they pay for being born helpless." And with this he kissed little Jane on both cheeks with evident satisfaction.

This bravado encouraged Uncle John to do likewise, but after the operation he looked sheepish and awkward, as if he felt that he had taken an unfair advantage of the wee lady.

"She seems very red, Louise," he remarked, to cover his embarrassment.

"Oh, no, Uncle! Everyone says she's the whitest baby of her age they ever saw. She's only five months old, remember."

"Dear me; how very young."

"But she's getting older every day," said Arthur, coming in from the garage. "What do you folks think of her, anyhow?"

The rhapsodies were fairly bewildering, yet very pleasant to the young father and mother. While they continued, Mildred Travers quietly took the child from Louise and tenderly bent over it. Only the major noted the little scene that ensued.

The eyes of the dark-skinned Mexican girl flashed sudden fire. She pulled Mildred's sleeve and then fell back discomfited as the cold, fathomless eyes of the trained nurse met her own. For an instant the girl stood irresolute; then with a quick, unexpected motion she tore the infant from Mildred's arms and rushed into the house with it.

Arthur, noticing this last action, laughed lightly. The major frowned. Mildred folded her arms and stood in the background unmoved and unobtrusive. Louise was chatting volubly with her two cousins.

"Was that the same Mexican girl who fed the baby chile con carne?" inquired Uncle John anxiously.

"Mercy, no!" cried Arthur. "What ever put such an idea into your head?"

"I believe the major suggested it," replied the little man. "Anyhow, it was something hot, so Louise wrote."

"Oh, yes; when Toodlums had the colic. It was some queer Mexican remedy, but I'm confident it saved the child's life. The girl is a treasure."

Uncle John coughed and glanced uneasily at Miss Travers, who pretended not to have overheard this conversation. But the major was highly amused and decided it was a good joke on Mr. Merrick. It was so good a joke

17

that it might serve as a basis for many cutting remarks in future discussions. His brother-in-law was so seldom guilty of an error in judgment that Major Doyle, who loved to oppose him because he was so fond of him, hailed Uncle John's present predicament with pure joy.

Louise created a welcome diversion by ushering them all into the house and through the stately rooms to the open court, where a luncheon table was set beneath the shade of the palms.

Here was the baby again, with the Mexican girl, Inez, hugging it defiantly to her bosom as she sat upon a stone bench.

Between the infant, the excitement of arrival and admiration for the Weldon establishment, so far surpassing their most ardent anticipations, Beth and Patsy had little desire for food. Uncle John and the major, however, did ample justice to an excellent repast, which was served by two more Mexican maids.

"Do you employ only Mexicans for servants?" inquired Uncle John, when finally the men were left alone to smoke while the girls, under Louise's guidance, explored the house.

"Only Mexicans, except for the Chinese cook," replied Arthur. "It is impossible to get American help and the Japs I won't have. Some of the ranch hands have been on the place for years, but the house servants I hired after I come here."

"A lazy lot, eh?" suggested the major.

"Quite right, sir. But I find them faithful and easy to manage. You will notice that I keep two or three times as many house servants as a similar establishment would require in the east; but they are content with much smaller wages. It's the same way on the ranch. Yet without the Mexicans the help problem would be a serious one out here."

"Does the ranch pay?" asked Mr. Merrick.

"I haven't been here long enough to find out," answered Arthur, with a smile. "So far, I've done all the paying. We shall harvest a big orange crop next month, and in time the olives will mature; but I've an idea the expenses will eat up the receipts, by the end of the year."

"No money in a California ranch, eh?"

"Why, some of my neighbors are making fortunes, I hear; but they are experienced ranchers. On the other hand, my next neighbor at the north is nearly bankrupt, because he's a greenhorn from the east. Some time, when I've learned the game, I hope to make this place something more than a plaything."

"You'll stay here, then?" asked the major, with astonishment. "It's the most delightful country on earth, for a residence. You'll admit that, sir, when you know it better."

Meantime the baggage wagon arrived and Patsy and Beth, having picked out their rooms, began to unpack and "settle" in their new quarters.

CHAPTER IV—LITTLE JANE'S TWO NURSES

Louise had been considerably puzzled to account for the presence of the strange girl in Uncle John's party. At first she did not know whether to receive Mildred Travers as an equal or a dependent. Not until the three nieces were seated together in Louise's own room, exchanging girlish confidences, was Mildred's status clearly defined to the young mother.

"You see," explained Patsy, "Uncle John was dreadfully worried over the baby. When you wrote of that terrible time the dear little one had with the colic, and how you were dependent on a Mexican girl who fed the innocent lamb some horrid hot stuff, Uncle declared it was a shame to imperil such a precious life, and that you must have a thoroughly competent nurse."

"But," said Louise, quite bewildered, "I'm afraid you don't understand that—"

"And so," broke in Beth, "I told him I knew of a perfect jewel of a trained nurse, who knows as much as most doctors and could guard the baby from a thousand dangers. I'd watched her care for one of our poor girls who was knocked down by an automobile and badly injured, and Mildred was so skillful and sympathetic that she quite won my heart. I wasn't sure, at first, she'd come way out to California, to stay, but when I broached the subject she cried out: 'Thank heaven!' in such a heart-felt, joyous tone that I was greatly relieved. So we brought her along, and—"

"Really, Beth, I don't need her," protested Louise. "The Mexicans are considered the best nurses in the world, and Inez is perfectly devoted to baby and worships her most sinfully. I got her from a woman who formerly employed her as a nurse and she gave Inez a splendid recommendation. Both Arthur and I believe she saved baby's life by her prompt action when the colic caught her."

"But the hot stuff!" cried Patsy.

"It might have ruined baby's stomach for life," asserted Beth.

"No; it's a simple Mexican remedy that is very efficient. Perhaps, in my anxiety, I wrote more forcibly than the occasion justified," admitted Louise; "but I have every confidence in Inez."

The girls were really dismayed and frankly displayed their chagrin. Louise laughed at them.

"Never mind," she said; "it's just one of dear Uncle John's blunders in trying to be good to me; so let's endeavor to wiggle out of the hole as gracefully as possible."

"I don't see how you'll do it," confessed Patsy. "Here's Mildred, permanently engaged and all expenses paid."

"She is really a superior person, as you'll presently discover," added Beth. "I've never dared question her as to her family history, but I venture to say she is well born and with just as good antecedents as we have—perhaps better."

"She's very quiet and undemonstrative," said Patsy musingly.

"Naturally, being a trained nurse. I liked her face," said Louise, "but her eyes puzzle me."

"They are her one unfortunate feature," Beth agreed.

"They're cold," said Patsy; "that's the trouble. You never get *into* her eyes, somehow. They repel you."

"I never look at them," said Beth. "Her mouth is sweet and sensitive and her facial expression pleasant. She moves as gracefully and silently as—as—"

"As a cat," suggested Patsy.

"And she is acquainted with all the modern methods of nursing, although she's done a lot of hospital work, too."

"Well," said Louise, reflectively, "I'll talk it over with Arthur and see what we can do. Perhaps baby needs two nurses. We can't discharge Inez, for Toodlums is even more contented with her than with me; but I admit it will be a satisfaction to have so thoroughly competent a nurse as Miss Travers at hand in case of emergency. And, above all else, I don't want to hurt dear Uncle John's feelings."

She did talk it over with Arthur, an hour later, and her boy husband declared he had "sized up the situation" the moment he laid eyes on Mildred at the depot. They owed a lot to Uncle John, he added, and the most graceful thing they could do, under the circumstances, was to instal Miss Travers as head nurse and retain Inez as her assistant.

"The chances are," said Arthur laughingly, "that the Mexican girl will have most of the care of Toodlums, as she does now, while the superior will remain content to advise Inez and keep a general supervision over the nursery. So fix it up that way, Louise, and everybody will be happy."

Uncle John was thanked so heartily for his thoughtfulness by the young couple that his kindly face glowed with satisfaction, and then Louise began the task of reconciling the two nurses to the proposed arrangement and defining the duties of each. Mildred Travers inclined her head graciously and said it was an admirable arrangement and quite satisfactory to her. But Inez listened sullenly and her dark eyes glowed with resentment.

"You not trust me more, then?" she added.

"Oh, yes, Inez; we trust you as much as ever," Louise assured her.

"Then why you hire this strange woman?"

"She is a present to us, from my Uncle John, who came this morning. He didn't know you were here, you see, or he would not have brought her."

Inez remained unmollified.

"Miss Travers is a very skillful baby doctor," continued Louise, "and she can mend broken bones, cure diseases and make the sick well."

Inez nodded.

"I know. A witch-woman," she said in a whisper. "You can trust me señora, but you cannot trust her. No witch-woman can be trusted."

Louise smiled but thought best not to argue the point farther. Inez went back to the nursery hugging Toodlums as jealously as if she feared some one would snatch the little one from her arms.

Next morning Mildred said to Beth, in whom she confided most:

"The Mexican girl does not like me. She is devotedly attached to the baby and fears I will supplant her."

"That is true," admitted Beth, who had conceived the same idea; "but you mustn't mind her, Mildred. The poor thing's only half civilized and doesn't understand our ways very well. What do you think of little Jane?"

"I never knew a sweeter, healthier or more contented baby. She smiles and sleeps perpetually and seems thoroughly wholesome. Were she to remain in her present robust condition there would be little need of my services, I assure you. But—"

"But what?" asked Beth anxiously, as the nurse hesitated.

"All babies have their ills, and little Jane cannot escape them. The rainy season is approaching and dampness is trying to infants. There will be months of moisture, and then—I shall be needed."

"Have you been in California before?" asked Beth, impressed by Mildred's positive assertion.

The girl hesitated a moment, looking down.

"I was born here," she said in low, tense tones.

"Indeed! Why, I thought all the white people in California came from the east. I had no idea there could be such a thing as a white native."

Mildred smiled with her lips. Her imperturbable eyes never smiled.

"I am only nineteen, in spite of my years of training and hard work," she said, a touch of bitterness in her voice. "My father came here nearly thirty years ago."

"To Southern California?"

"Yes."

"Did you live near here, then?"

Mildred looked around her.

"I have been in this house often, as a girl," she said slowly. "Señor Cristoval was—an acquaintance of my father."

Beth stared at her, greatly interested.

"How strange!" she exclaimed. "You cannot be far from your own family, then," she added.

Mildred shivered a little, twisting her fingers nervously together. She was indeed sensitive, despite that calm, repellent look in her eyes.

"I hope," she said, evading Beth's remark, "to be of real use to this dear baby, whom I already love. The Mexican girl, Inez, is well enough as a caretaker, but her judgment could not be trusted in emergencies. These Mexicans lose their heads easily and in crises are liable to do more harm than good. Mrs. Weldon's arrangement is an admirable one and I confess it relieves me of much drudgery and confinement. I shall keep a watchful supervision over my charge and be prepared to meet any emergency."

Beth was not wholly satisfied with this interview. Mildred had told her just enough to render her curious, but had withheld any information as to how a California girl happened to be in New York working as a trained nurse. She remembered the girl's fervent exclamation: "Thank heaven!" when asked if she would go to Southern California, to a ranch called El Cajon, to take care of a new baby. Beth judged from this that Mildred was eager to get back home again; yet she had evaded any reference to her family or former friends, and since her arrival had expressed no wish to visit them.

24

There was something strange and unaccountable about the affair, and for this reason Beth refrained from mentioning to her cousins that Mildred Travers was a Californian by birth and was familiar with the scenes around El Cajon ranch and even with the old house itself. Perhaps some day the girl would tell her more, when she would be able to relate the whole story to Patsy and Louise.

Of course the new arrivals were eager to inspect the orange and olive groves, so on the day following that of their arrival the entire party prepared to join Arthur Weldon in a tramp over the three hundred acre ranch.

A little way back of the grounds devoted to the residence and gardens began the orange groves, the dark green foliage just now hung thick with fruit, some green, some pale yellow and others of that deep orange hue which denotes full maturity. "They consider five acres of oranges a pretty fair ranch, out here," said the young proprietor; "but I have a hundred and ten acres of bearing trees. It will take a good many freight cars to carry my oranges to the eastern markets."

"And what a job to pick them all!" exclaimed Patsy.

"We don't pick them," said Arthur. "I sell the crop on the trees and the purchaser sends a crew of men who gather the fruit in quick order. They are taken to big warehouses and sorted into sizes, wrapped and packed and loaded onto cars. That is a separate branch of the business with which we growers have nothing to do."

Between the orange and the olive groves, and facing a little lane, they came upon a group of adobe huts—a little village in itself. Many children were playing about the yards, while several stalwart Mexicans lounged in the shade quietly smoking their eternal cigarettes. Women appeared in the doorways, shading their eyes with their hands as they curiously examined the approaching strangers.

Only one man, a small, wiry fellow with plump brown cheeks and hair and beard of snowy whiteness, detached himself from the group and advanced to meet his master. Removing his wide sombrero he made a sweeping bow, a gesture so comical that Patsy nearly laughed aloud.

"This is Miguel Zaloa, the ranchero, who has charge of all my men," said Arthur. Then, addressing the man, he asked: "Any news, Miguel?"

"Ever'thing all right, Meest Weld," replied the ranchero, his bright eyes earnestly fixed upon his employer's face. "Some pardon, señor; but—Mees Jane is well?"

"Quite well, thank you, Miguel."

"Mees Jane," said the man, shyly twirling his hat in his hands as he cast an upward glance at the young ladies, "ees cherub young lade; much love an' beaut'ful. Ees not?"

"She's a dear," replied Patsy, with ready sympathy for the sentiment and greatly pleased to find the man so ardent an admirer of the baby.

"Ever'bod' love Mees Jane," continued old Miguel, simply. "Since she have came, sun ees more bright, air ees more good, tamale ees more sweet. Will Inez bring Mees Jane to see us to-day, Meest Weld?"

"Perhaps so," laughed Arthur; and then, as he turned to lead them to the olive trees, Louise, blushing prettily at the praise bestowed upon her darling, pressed a piece of shining silver into old Miguel's hand—which he grasped with alacrity and another low bow.

"No doubt he's right about little Jane," remarked the major, when they had passed beyond earshot, "but I've a faint suspicion the old bandit praised her in order to get the money."

"Oh, no!" cried Louise; "he's really sincere. It is quite wonderful how completely all our Mexicans are wrapped up in baby. If Inez doesn't wheel the baby-cab over to the quarters every day, they come to the house in droves to inquire if 'Mees Jane' is well. Their love for her is almost pathetic."

"Don't the fellows ever work?" inquired Uncle John.

"Yes, indeed," said Arthur. "Have you any fault to find with the condition of this ranch? As compared with many others it is a model of perfection. At daybreak the mules are cultivating the earth around the trees; when the sun gets low the irrigating begins. We keep the harrows and the pumps busy every day. But during the hours when the sun shines brightest the Mexicans do not love to work, and it is policy—so long as they accomplish their tasks—to allow them to choose their own hours for labor."

"They seem a shiftless lot," said the major.

"They're as good as their average type. But some—old Miguel, for instance—are better than the ordinary. Miguel is really a clever and industrious fellow. He has lived here practically all his life and knows intimately every tree on the place."

"Did he serve the old Spanish don—Cristoval?" asked Beth.

"Yes; and his father before him. I've often wondered how old Miguel is. According to his own story he must be nearly a hundred; but that's absurd. Anyhow, he's a faithful, capable fellow, and rules the others with the rigor of an autocrat. I don't know what I should do without him."

"You seem to have purchased a lot of things with this ranch," observed Uncle John. "A capital old mansion, a band of trained servants, and—a ghost."

"Oh, yes!" exclaimed Louise. "Major, did the ghost bother you last night?"

"Not to my knowledge," said the old soldier. "I was too tired to keep awake, you know; therefore his ghostship could not have disturbed me without being unusually energetic."

"Have you ever seen the ghost, Louise?" inquired Patsy.

"No, dear, nor even heard it. But Arthur has. It's in the blue room, you know, near Arthur's study—one of the prettiest rooms in the house."

"That's why we gave it to the major," added Arthur. "Once or twice, when I've been sitting in the study, at about midnight, reading and smoking my pipe, I've heard some queer noises coming from the blue room; but I attribute them to rats. These old houses are full of the pests and we can't manage to get rid of them."

"I imagine the walls are not all solid," explained Louise, "for some of those on the outside are from six to eight feet in thickness, and it would be folly to make them of solid adobe."

"As for that, adobe costs nothing," said Arthur, "and it would be far cheaper to make a solid wall than a hollow one. But between the blocks are a lot of spaces favored as residences by our enemies the rats, and there they are safe from our reach."

"But the ghost?" demanded Patsy.

"Oh, the ghost exists merely in the minds of the simple Mexicans, over there at the quarters. Most of them were here when that rascally old Cristoval died, and no money would hire one of them to sleep in the house. You see, they feared and hated the old fellow, who doubtless treated them cruelly. That is why we had to get our house servants from a distance, and even then we had some difficulty in quieting their fears when they heard the ghost tales. Little Inez," added Louise, "is especially superstitious, and I'm sure if she were not so devoted to baby she would have left us weeks ago."

"Inez told me this morning," said Beth, "that the major must be a very brave man and possessed some charm that protected him from ghosts, or he would never dare sleep in the blue room."

"I have a charm," declared the major, gravely, "and it's just common sense."

But now they were among the graceful, broad-spreading olives, at this season barren of fruit but very attractive in their gray-green foliage. Arthur had to explain all about olive culture to the ignorant Easterners and he did this with much satisfaction because he had so recently acquired the knowledge himself.

"I can see," said Uncle John, "that your ranch is to be a great gamble. In good years, you win; a crop failure will cost you a fortune."

"True," admitted the young man; "but an absolute crop failure is unknown in this section. Some years are better than others, but all are good years."

It was quite a long tramp, but a very pleasant one, and by the time they returned to the house everyone was ready for luncheon, which awaited them in the shady court, beside the splashing fountain. Patsy and Beth demanded the baby, so presently Inez came with little Jane, and Mildred Travers followed after. The two nurses did not seem on very friendly terms, for the Mexican girl glared fiercely at her rival and Mildred returned a basilisk stare that would have confounded anyone less defiant.

This evident hostility amused Patsy, annoyed Beth and worried Louise; but the baby was impartial. From her seat on Inez' lap little Jane stretched out her tiny hands to Mildred, smiling divinely, and the nurse took the child in spite of Inez' weak resistance, fondling the little one lovingly. There was a sharp contrast between Mildred's expert and adroit handling of the child and Inez' tender awkwardness, and this was so evident that all present noticed it.

Perhaps Inez herself felt this difference as, sullen and jealous, she eyed the other intently. Then little Jane transferred her favors to her former nurse and held out her hands to Inez. With a cry that was half a sob the girl caught the baby in her arms and held it so closely that Patsy had hard work to make her give it up.

By the time Uncle John had finished his lunch both Patsy and Beth had taken turns holding the fascinating "Toodlums," and now the latter plunged Jane into Mr. Merrick's lap and warned him to be very careful.

Uncle John was embarrassed but greatly delighted. He cooed and clucked to the baby until it fairly laughed aloud with glee, and then he made faces until the infant became startled and regarded him with grave suspicion.

"If you've done making an old fool of yourself, sir," said the major severely, "you'll oblige me by handing over my niece."

"*Your* niece!" was the indignant reply; "she's nothing of the sort. Jane is *my* niece."

"No more than mine," insisted the major; "and you're worrying her. Will you hand her over, you selfish man, or must I take her by force?"

Uncle John reluctantly submitted to the divorce and the major handled the baby as if she had been glass.

"Ye see," he remarked, lapsing slightly into his Irish brogue, as he was apt to do when much interested, "I've raised a daughter meself, which John Merrick hasn't, and I know the ways of the wee women. They know very well when a friend has 'em, and—Ouch! Leg-go, I say!"

Little Jane had his grizzly moustache fast in two chubby fists and the major's howls aroused peals of laughter.

Uncle John nearly rolled from his chair in an ecstacy of delight and he could have shaken Mildred Travers for releasing the grip of the baby fingers and rescuing the major from torture.

"Laugh, ye satyr!" growled the major, wiping the tears from his own eyes. "It's lucky you have no hair nor whiskers—any more than an egg—or you'd be writhing in agony before now." He turned to look wonderingly at the crowing baby in Mildred's arms. "It's a female Sandow!" he averred. "The grip of her hands is something marvelous!"

CHAPTER V—INEZ THREATENS

"Yes," said Louise, a week later, "we all make fools of ourselves over Toodlums, Really, girls, Jane is a very winning baby. I don't say that because I'm her mother, understand. If she were anyone else's baby, I'd say the same thing."

"Of course," agreed Patsy. "I don't believe such a baby was ever before born. She's so happy, and sweet, and—and—"

"And comfortable," said Beth. "Indeed, Jane is a born sorceress; she bewitches everyone who beholds her dear dimpled face. This is an impartial opinion, you know; I'd say the same thing if I were not her adoring auntie."

"It's true," Patsy declared. "Even the Mexicans worship her. And Mildred Travers—the sphinx—whose blood I am sure is ice-water, displays a devotion for baby that is absolutely amazing. I don't blame her, you know, for it must be a real delight to care for such a fairy. I'm surprised, Louise, that you can bear to have baby out of your sight so much of the time."

Louise laughed lightly.

"I'm not such an unfeeling mother as you think," she answered. "I know just where baby is every minute and she is never out of my thoughts. However, with two nurses, both very competent, to care for Toodlums, I do not think it necessary to hold her in my lap every moment."

Here Uncle John and the major approached the palm, under which the three nieces were sitting, and Mr. Merrick exclaimed:

"I'll bet a cookie you were talking of baby Jane."

"You'd win, then," replied Patsy. "There's no other topic of conversation half so delightful."

"Jane," observed the major, musingly, as he seated himself in a rustic chair. "A queer name for a baby, Louise. Whatever possessed you to burden the poor infant with it?"

"Burden? Nonsense, Major! It's a charming name," cried Patsy.

"She is named after poor Aunt Jane," said Louise.

A silence somewhat awkward followed.

"My sister Jane," remarked Uncle John gravely, "was in some respects an admirable woman."

"And in many others detestable," said Beth in frank protest. "The only good thing I can remember about Aunt Jane," she added, "is that she brought us three girls together, when we had previously been almost unaware of one anothers' existence. And she made us acquainted with Uncle John."

"Then she did us another favor," added Patsy. "She died."

"Poor Aunt Jane!" sighed Louise. "I wish I could say something to prove that I revere her memory. Had the baby been a boy, its name would have been John; but being a girl I named her for Uncle John's sister—the highest compliment I could conceive."

Uncle John nodded gratefully. "I wasn't especially fond of Jane, myself," said he, "but it's a family name and I'm glad you gave it to baby."

"Jane Merrick," said the major, "was very cruel to Patsy and to me, and so I'm sorry you gave her name to baby."

"Always contrary, eh?" returned Uncle John, with a tolerant smile, for he was in no wise disturbed by this adverse criticism of his defunct sister—a criticism that in fact admitted little argument. "But it occurs to me that the most peculiar thing about this name is that you three girls, who were once Aunt Jane's nieces, are now Niece Jane's aunts!"

"Except me," smiled Louise. "I'm happy to claim a closer relationship. But returning to our discussion of Aunt Jane. She was really instrumental in making our fortunes as well as in promoting our happiness, so I have no regret because I made baby her namesake."

"The name of Jane," said Patsy, "is in itself beautiful, because it is simple and old-fashioned. Now that it is connected with my chubby niece it will derive a new and added luster."

"Quite true," declared Uncle John.

"Where is Arthur?" inquired the major.

"Writing his weekly batch of letters," replied Arthur's wife. "When they are ready he is to drive us all over to town in the big car, and we have planned to have lunch there and to return home in the cool of the evening. Will that program please our guests?"

All voiced their approval and presently Arthur appeared with his letters and bade them get ready for the ride, while he brought out the car. He always drove the machine himself, as no one on the place was competent to act as chauffeur; but he managed it admirably and enjoyed driving.

Louise went to the nursery to kiss little Jane. The baby lay in her crib, fast asleep. Near her sat Mildred Travers, reading a book. Crouched in the window-seat was Inez, hugging her knees and gazing moodily out into the garden.

The nursery was in the East Wing, facing the courtyard but also looking upon the rose garden, its one deep-set window being near a corner of the room. On one side it connected with a small chamber used by Inez, which occupied half the depth of the wing and faced the garden. The other half of the space was taken by a small sewing-room letting out upon the court.

At the opposite side of little Jane's nursery was a roomy chamber which had been given up to Mildred, and still beyond this were the rooms occupied by Arthur and Louise, all upon the ground floor. By this arrangement the baby had a nurse on either side and was only one room removed from its parents.

This wing was said to be the oldest part of the mansion, a fact attested by the great thickness of the walls. Just above was the famous blue room occupied by the major, where ghosts were supposed at times to hold their revels. Yet, despite its clumsy construction, the East Wing was cheery and pleasant in all its rooms and sunlight flooded it the year round.

After the master and mistress had driven away to town with their guests, Inez sat for a time by the window, still motionless save for an occasional wicked glance over her shoulder at Mildred, who read placidly as she rocked to and fro in her chair. The presence of the American nurse seemed to oppress the girl, for not a semblance of friendship had yet developed between the two; so presently Inez rose and glided softly out into the court, leaving Mildred to watch the sleeping baby.

She took the path that led to the Mexican quarters and ten minutes later entered the hut where Bella, the skinny old hag who was the wife to Miguel Zaloa, was busy with her work.

"Ah, Inez. But where ees Mees Jane?" was the eager inquiry.

Inez glanced around to find several moustached faces in the doorway. Every dark, earnest eye repeated the old woman's question. The girl shrugged her shoulders.

"She is care for by the new nurse, Meeldred. I left her sleeping."

"Who sleeps, Inez?" demanded the aged Miguel. "Ees it the new nurse, or Mees Jane?"

"Both, perhap." She laughed scornfully and went out to the shed that connected two of the adobe dwellings and served as a shady lounging place. Here a group quickly formed around her, including those who followed from the hut.

"I shall kill her, some day," declared the girl, showing her gleaming teeth. "What right have she to come an' take our baby?"

Miguel stroked his white moustache reflectively.

"Ees this Meeldred good to Mees Jane?" he asked.

"When anyone looks, yes," replied Inez reluctantly. "She fool even baby, some time, who laugh at her. But poor baby do not know. I know. This Meeldred ees a devil!" she hissed.

The listening group displayed no emotion at this avowal. They eyed the girl attentively, as if expecting to hear more. But Inez, having vented her spite, now sulked.

"Where she came from?" asked Miguel, the recognized spokesman.

"Back there. New York," tossing her head in an easterly direction.

"Why she come?" continued the old man.

"The little mans with no hair—Meest Merrick—he think I not know about babies. He think this girl who learns babies in school, an' from books, know more than me who has care for many baby—but for none like our Mees Jane. Mees Jane ees angel!"

They all nodded in unison, approving her assertion.

"Eet ees not bad thought, that," remarked old Bella. "Books an' schools ees good to teach wisdom."

"Pah! Not for babies," objected her husband, shaking his head. "Book an' school can not grow orange, either. To do a thing many time ees to know it better than a book can know."

"Besides," said Inez, "this Meeldred ees witch-woman."

"Yes?"

"I know it. She come from New York. But yesterday she say to me: 'Let us wheel leetle Jane to the live oak at Burney's.' How can she know there is live oak at Burney's? Then, the first day she come, she say: 'Take baby's milk into vault under your room an' put on stone shelf to keep cool.' I, who live here, do not know of such a vault. She show me some stone steps in one corner, an' she push against stone wall. Then wall open like door, an' I find vault. But how she know it, unless she is witch-woman?"

There was a murmur of astonishment. Old Miguel scratched his head as if puzzled.

"I, too, know about thees vault," said he; "but then, eet ees I know all of the old house, as no one else know. Once I live there with Señor Cristoval. But how can thees New York girl know?"

There was no answer. Merely puzzled looks.

"What name has she, Inez?" suddenly asked Miguel.

"Travers. Meeldred Travers."

The old man thought deeply and then shook his head with a sigh.

"In seexty year there be no Travers near El Cajon," he asserted. "I thought maybe she have been here before. But no. Even in old days there ees no Travers come here."

"There ees a Travers Ranch over at the north," asserted Bella.

"Eet ees a name; there be no Travers live there," declared Miguel, still with that puzzled look upon his plump features.

Inez laughed at him.

"She is witch-woman, I tell you. I know it! Look in her eyes, an' see."

The group of Mexicans moved uneasily. Old Miguel deliberately rolled a cigarette and lighted it.

"Thees woman I have not yet see," he announced, after due reflection. "But, if she ees witch-woman, eet ees bad for Mees Jane to be near her."

"That is what *I* say!" cried Inez eagerly. She spoke better English than the others. "She will bewitch my baby; she will make it sickly, so it will die!" And she wrung her hands in piteous misery.

The Mexicans exchanged frightened looks. Old Bella alone seemed unaffected.

"Mees Weld own her baby—not us," suggested Miguel's wife. "If Mees

Weld theenk thees girl is safe nurse, what have we to say—eh?"

"I say she shall not kill my baby!" cried Inez fiercely. "That is what *I* say, Bella. Before she do that, I kill thees Meeldred Travers."

Miguel examined the girl's face intently.

"You are fool, Inez," he asserted. "It ees bad to keel anything—even thees New York witch-woman. Be compose an' keep watch. Nothing harm Mees Jane if you watch. Where are your folks, girl?"

"Live in San Diego," replied Inez, again sullen.

"Once I know your father. He ees good man, but drink too much. If you make quarrel about thees new nurse, you get sent home. Then you lose Mees Jane. So keep compose, an' watch. If you see anything wrong, come to me an' tell it. That ees best."

Inez glanced around the group defiantly, but all nodded approval of old Miguel's advice. She rose from the bench where she was seated, shrugged her shoulders disdainfully and walked away without a word.

CHAPTER VI—A DINNER WITH THE NEIGHBORS

Escondido, the nearest town and post office to El Cajon Ranch, is a quaint little place with a decided Mexican atmosphere. Those California inhabitants whom we call, for convenience, "Mexicans," are not all natives of Mexico, by any means. Most of them are a mixed breed derived from the early Spanish settlers and the native Indian tribes—both alike practically extinct in this locality—and have never stepped foot in Mexican territory, although the boundary line is not far distant. Because the true Mexican is generally a similar admixture of Indian and Spaniard, it is customary to call these Californians by the same appellation. The early Spaniards left a strong impress upon this state, and even in the newly settled districts the Spanish architecture appropriately prevails, as typical of a semi-tropical country which owed its first civilizing influences to old Spain.

The houses of Escondido are a queer mingling of modern bungalows and antique adobe dwellings. Even the business street shows many adobe structures. A quiet, dreamy little town, with a comfortable hotel and excellent stores, it is much frequented by the wealthy ranchers in its neighborhood.

After stopping at the post office, Arthur drove down a little side street to a weather-beaten, unprepossessing building which bore the word "Restaurant" painted in dim white letters upon its one window. Here he halted the machine.

"Oh," said Beth, drawing a long breath. "Is this one of your little jokes, Arthur?"

"A joke? Didn't we come for luncheon, then?"

"We did, and I'm ravenous," said Patsy. "But you informed us that there is a good hotel here, on the main street."

"So there is," admitted Arthur; "but it's like all hotels. Now, this is—

different. If you're hungry; if you want a treat—something out of the ordinary —just follow me."

Louise was laughing at their doubting expressions and this care-free levity led them to obey their host's injunction. Then the dingy door opened and out stepped a young fellow whom the girls decided must be either a cowboy or a clever imitation of one.

He seemed very young—a mere boy—for all his stout little form. He was bareheaded and a shock of light, tow-colored hair was in picturesque disarray. A blue flannel shirt, rolled up at the sleeves, a pair of drab corduroy trousers and rough shoes completed his attire. Pausing awkwardly in the doorway, he first flushed red and then advanced boldly to shake Arthur's hand.

"Why, Weldon, this is an unexpected pleasure," he exclaimed in a pleasant voice that belied his rude costume, for its tones were well modulated and cultured. "I've been trying to call you up for three days, but something is wrong with the line. How's baby?"

This last question was addressed to Louise, who shook the youth's hand cordially.

"Baby is thriving finely," she reported, and then introduced her friends to Mr. Rudolph Hahn, who, she explained, was one of their nearest neighbors.

"We almost crowd the Weldons," he said, "for our house is only five miles distant from theirs; so we've been getting quite chummy since they moved to El Cajon. Helen—that's my wife, you know—is an humble worshiper at the shrine of Miss Jane Weldon, as we all are, in fact."

"Your wife!" cried Patsy in surprise.

He laughed.

"You think I'm an infant, only fit to play with Jane," said he; "but I assure you I could vote, if I wanted to—which I don't. I think, sir," turning to Uncle John, "that my father knows you quite well."

"Why, surely you're not the son of Andy Hahn, the steel king?"

"I believe they do give him that royal title; but Dad is only a monarch in finance, and when he visits my ranch he's as much a boy as his son."

"It scarcely seems possible," declared Mr. Merrick, eyeing the rough costume wonderingly but also with approval. "How long have you lived out here?"

"Six years, sir. I'm an old inhabitant. Weldon, here, has only been alive for six months."

"Alive?"

"Of course. One breathes, back east, but only lives in California."

During the laughter that followed this enthusiastic epigram Arthur ushered the party into the quaint Spanish restaurant. The room was clean and neat, despite the fact that the floor was strewn with sawdust and the tables covered with white oilcloth. An anxious-eyed, dapper little man with a foreign face and manner greeted them effusively and asked in broken English their commands.

Arthur ordered the specialties of the house. "These friends, Castro, are from the far East, and I've told them of your famous cuisine. Don't disappoint them."

"May I join you?" asked Rudolph Hahn. "I wish I'd brought Nell over to-day; she'd have been delighted with this meeting. But we didn't know you were coming. That confounded telephone doesn't reach you at all."

"I'm going over to the office to see about that telephone," said Arthur. "I believe I'll do the errand while Castro is preparing his compounds. I'm always uneasy when the telephone is out of order."

"You ought to be," said Rudolph, "with that blessed baby in the house. It might save you thirty precious minutes in getting a doctor."

"Does your line work?" asked Louise.

"Yes; it seems to get all connections but yours. So I imagine something is wrong with your phone, or near the house."

"I'll have them send a repair man out at once," said Arthur, and departed for the telephone office, accompanied by his fellow rancher.

While they were gone Louise told them something of young Hahn's history. He had eloped, at seventeen years of age, with his father's stenographer, a charming girl of eighteen who belonged to one of the best families in Washington. Old Hahn was at first furious and threatened to disinherit the boy, but when he found the young bride's family still more furious and preparing to annul the marriage on the grounds of the groom's youth, the great financier's mood changed and he whisked the pair off to California and bought for them a half-million-dollar ranch, where they had lived for six years a life of unalloyed bliss. Having no children of their own, the Hahns were devoted to little Jane and it was Rudolph who had given the baby the sobriquet of "Toodlums." At almost any time, night or day, the Hahn automobile was liable to arrive at El Cajon for a sight of the baby.

"Rudolph—we call him 'Dolph,' you know—has not a particle of business instinct," said Louise, "so he will never be able to take his father's place in the financial world. And he runs his ranch so extravagantly that it costs the pater a small fortune every year. Yet they are agreeable neighbors, artless and unconventional as children, and surely the great Hahn fortune won't suffer much through their inroads."

When Arthur returned he brought with him still another neighboring ranchman, an enormous individual fully six feet tall and broad in proportion, who fairly filled the doorway as he entered. This man was about thirty years of age, stern of feature and with shaggy brows that overhung a pair of peaceful blue eyes which ought to have been set in the face of some child. This gave him a whimsical look that almost invariably evoked a smile when anyone observed him for the first time. He walked with a vigorous, aggressive stride and handled his big body with consummate grace and ease. His bow, when Arthur introduced him, was that of an old world cavalier.

41

"Here is another of our good friends for you to know. He's our neighbor at the north and is considered the most enterprising orange grower in all California," announced Weldon, with a chuckle that indicated he had said something funny.

"Lemon," said the man, speaking in such a shrill, high-pitched tenor voice that the sound was positively startling, coming from so massive a chest.

"I meant lemon," Arthur hastened to say. "Permit me to introduce Mr. Bulwer Runyon, formerly of New York but now the pride of the Pacific coast, where his superb oranges—"

"Lemons," piped the high, childish voice.

"Whose lemons are the sourest and—and—juiciest ever grown."

"What there are of them," added the man in a wailing tenor.

"We are highly honored to meet Mr. Bulwer Runyon," said the major, noticing that the girls were for once really embarrassed how to greet this new acquaintance.

"Out here," remarked Dolph Hahn, with a grin, "we drop the handle to his name and call him 'Bul Run' for short. Sounds sort of patriotic, you know, and it's not inappropriate."

"You wrong me," said the big rancher, squeaking the words cheerfully but at the same time frowning in a way that might well have terrified a pirate. "I'm not a bull and I don't run. It's enough exertion to walk. Therefore I ride. My new car is equipped with one of those remarkable—"

"Pardon me; we will not discuss your new car, if you please," said Arthur. "We wish to talk of agreeable things. The marvelous Castro is concocting some of his mysterious dishes and we wish you to assist us in judging their merits."

"I shall be glad to, for I'm pitifully hungry," said the tenor voice. "I had breakfast at seven, you know—like a working man—and the ride over here in my new six-cylinder machine, which has a wonderful—"

"Never mind the machine, please. Forget it, and try to be sociable," begged Dolph.

"How is the baby, Mrs. Weldon?"

"Well and hearty, Bulwer," replied Louise. "Why haven't you been to see little Jane lately?"

"I heard you had company," said Mr. Runyon; "and the last time I came I stayed three days and forgot all about my ranch. I've made a will, Mrs. Weldon."

"A will! You're not going to die, I hope?"

"I join you in that hope, most fervently, for I'd hate to leave the new machine and its—"

"Go on, Bulwer."

"But life is fleeting, and no one knows just when it'll get to the end of its fleet. Therefore, as I love the baby better than any other object on earth—animate or inanimate—except—"

"Never mind your new car."

He sighed.

"Therefore, Mrs. Weldon, I've made Jane my heiress."

"Oh, Bul! Aren't you dreadfully in debt?"

"Yes'm."

"Is the place worth the mortgage?" inquired Arthur.

"Just about, although the money sharks don't think so. But all property out here is rapidly increasing in value," declared Runyon, earnestly, "so, if I can manage to hold on a while longer, Toodlums will inherit a—a—several fine lemon trees, at least."

Uncle John was delighted with the big fellow with the small voice. Even the major clapped Bul Run on the shoulder and said the sentiment did him credit, however big the mortgage might be.

By the time Castro brought in his first surprise—a delicious soup—a jovial and friendly party was gathered around the oilcloth board. Even the paper napkins could not dampen the joy of the occasion, or detract from the exquisite flavor of the broth.

The boyish Dolph bewailed anon the absence of his "Nell," who loved Castro's cookery above everything else, while every endeavor of Mr. Runyon to explain the self-starter on his new car was so adroitly headed off by his fellow ranchers that the poor fellow was in despair. The "lunch" turned out to be a seven course dinner and each course introduced such an enticing and unusual dish that every member of the party became an audacious gormandizer. None of the girls—except Louise—had ever tasted such concoctions before, or might even guess what many of them were composed of; but all agreed with Patsy when she energetically asserted that "Castro out-cheffed both Rector and Sherry."

"If only he would have tablecloths and napkins, and decent rugs upon the floor," added dainty Louise.

"Oh, that would ruin the charm of the place," protested Uncle John. "Don't suggest such a horror to Castro, Louise; at least until after we have returned to New York."

"I'll take you riding in my car," piped Runyon to Beth, who sat beside him. "I don't have to crank it, you know; I just—"

"Have you sold your orange crop yet?" asked Arthur.

"Lemons, sir!" said the other reproachfully. And the laugh that followed again prevented his explaining the self-starter.

The porch was shady and cool when they emerged from the feast room and Arthur Weldon, as host, proposed they sit on the benches with their coffee and cigars and have a social chat. But both Runyon and Hahn protested this delay. They suggested, instead, that all ride back to El Cajon and play with the baby, and so earnest were they in this desire that the proud young father and mother had not the grace to refuse.

Both men had their cars at the village garage and an hour later the procession started. Beth riding beside "Bul Run" and Patsy accompanying the jolly "Dolph."

"We must stop and pick up Nell," said the latter, "for she'd be mad as hops if I went to see Toodlums without her."

"I don't wonder," replied Patsy. "Isn't my niece a dear baby?"

"Never was one born like her. She's the only woman I ever knew who refuses to talk."

"She crows, though."

"To signify she agrees with everyone on every question; and her angelic smile is so genuine and constant that it gets to your heart in spite of all resistance."

"And she's so soft and mushy, as it were," continued Patsy enthusiastically; "but I suppose she'll outgrow that, in time."

Mrs. Helen Hahn, when the three automobiles drew up before her young husband's handsome residence, promptly agreed to join Rudolph in a visit to the baby. She proved to be a retiring and rather shy young woman, but she was very beautiful and her personality was most attractive. Both Patsy and Beth were delighted to find that Louise had so charming a neighbor, of nearly her own age.

Rudolph would not permit the party to proceed further until all had partaken of a refreshing glass of lemonade, and as this entailed more or less delay the sun was getting low as they traversed the five miles to El Cajon, traveling slowly that they might enjoy the exquisite tintings of the sky. Runyon, who was a bachelor, lived a few miles the other side of Arthur's ranch. All three ranches had at one time been part of the Spanish grant to the Cristovals, and while Arthur now possessed the old mansion, the greatest

45

number of acres had been acquired by Rudolph Hahn, who had preferred to build for himself and his bride a more modern residence.

CHAPTER VII—GONE!

The Weldons and their guests were greeted at their door by a maid, for there were no men among the house servants, and as Louise ushered the party into the living room she said to the girl:

"Ask Miss Travers to bring the baby here."

The maid departed and was gone so long that Louise started out to see why her order was not obeyed. She met the woman coming back with a puzzled face.

"Mees Traver not here, señora," she said.

"Then tell Inez to fetch the baby."

"Inez not here, señora," returned the woman.

"Indeed! Then where is baby?"

"Mees Jane not here, señora."

Louise rushed to the nursery, followed by Arthur, whose quick ears had overheard the statement. The young mother bent over the crib, the covers of which were thrown back as if the infant had been quickly caught up—perhaps from a sound sleep.

"Good gracious!" cried Louise, despairingly; "she's gone—my baby's gone!"

"Gone?" echoed Arthur, in a distracted tone. "What does it mean, Louise? Where can she be?"

A gentle hand was laid on his shoulder and Uncle John, who had followed them to the room, said soothingly:

"Don't get excited, my boy; there's nothing to worry about. Your two nurses have probably taken little Jane out for a ride."

"At this time of night?" exclaimed Louise. "Impossible!"

"It is merely twilight; they may have been delayed," replied Mr. Merrick.

"But the air grows chill at this hour, and—"

"And there is the baby-cab!" added Arthur, pointing to a corner.

Louise and her husband looked into one another's eyes and their faces grew rigid and white. Uncle John, noting their terror, spoke again.

"This is absurd," said he. "Two competent nurses, both devoted to little Jane, would not allow the baby to come to harm, I assure you."

"Where is she, then?" demanded Arthur.

"Hello; what's up?" called Patsy Doyle, entering the room with Beth to see what was keeping them from their guests.

"Baby's gone!" wailed Louise, falling into a chair promptly to indulge in a flood of tears.

"Gone? Nonsense," said Beth, gazing into the empty cradle. Then she put down her hand and felt of the bedding. It had no warmth. Evidently the child had been removed long ago.

"Before we give way to hysterics," advised Uncle John, striving to appear calm, "let us investigate this matter sensibly. Babies don't disappear mysteriously, in these days, I assure you."

"Question the servants," suggested Patsy.

"That's the idea," squeaked a high tenor voice, and there in the dim light stood big Bulwer Runyon, and with him little Rudolph and his wife Helen, all exhibiting astonished and disturbed countenances.

"I—I can't see any reason for worry, Louise, dear," remarked Mrs. Hahn, in a voice that trembled with agitation. "Not a soul on earth would harm that precious Jane."

Arthur turned to the maid.

"Send all the servants here," he commanded. "Every one of them, mind you!"

Presently they congregated in the roomy nursery, which had now been brilliantly lighted. There were five women—some old and some young, but all Mexicans—and a little withered Chinaman named Sing Fing, whose age was uncertain and whose yellow face seemed incapable of expression.

Uncle John, assisted at times by Rudolph and Arthur, did the questioning. Marcia had seen Miss Travers leave the house, alone, at about two o'clock, as if for a walk. She did not notice which way the nurse went nor whether she returned. Perhaps she wore a cloak; Marcia could not tell. The day was warm; doubtless Miss Travers had no wraps at all. A hat? Oh, no. She would have noticed a hat.

The only one who recollected seeing Inez was Eulalia, a chambermaid. She had observed Inez sitting in the court, in a despondent attitude, at about half past two. Yes; it might have been a little earlier; it was hard to remember. None of the house servants paid much attention to the nurses. They had their own duties to perform.

But the baby had not been seen at all; not since Inez had brought her in from her ride at noon. Then it was Miss Travers who had taken the child from the cab and with her disappeared into the nursery.

This report did not prove reassuring. Sing Fing announced that Miss Travers had prepared the baby's liquid food in the kitchen at half past twelve, but that neither she nor Inez had joined the other servants at luncheon. This last was not an unusual occurrence, it seemed, but taken in connection with the other circumstances it impressed the questioners as suspicious.

"Perhaps they are all at the Mexican quarters," exclaimed Patsy, with sudden inspiration.

Arthur and Rudolph immediately volunteered to investigate the quarters and started off on a run.

"It's all right, you know," consolingly panted Dolph, on the way. "The baby and her nurses can't be lost, strayed or stolen, so don't worry."

"Common sense urges me to agree with you," returned Arthur, "but there's certainly something mysterious about the disappearance."

"It won't be mysterious when we discover the reason, you know."

The men were all at work in the olive groves, but some of the women were in the huts and old Bella listened to Arthur's frantic questions with blank amazement, as did the others who hastily congregated.

"Thees morn," said Bella, "Inez bring Mees Jane here for little time—not long time. Then she takes her 'way again."

"While Inez here," said another woman, "I see that other—the American nurse—behind hedge, yonder, watching us."

"How you know that?" demanded Bella sharply, as she turned to the speaker.

"I know because she is stranger," was the calm reply. "Inez see her, too, an' that ees why Inez hurry away."

"Which way did she go?" asked Arthur, and they all pointed to the path that led to the house.

"It doesn't matter," suggested Dolph. "We know that both the nurses were in the house afterward. The main point is that the baby is not here."

As they started to return they came face to face with old Miguel. The shadow was deep beneath the trees but there was no mistaking the Mexican's snow-white hair.

"Have you seen baby?" demanded Weldon eagerly.

Miguel stared at them. He came nearer, putting his face close to his master's, and stared harder.

"Mees Jane? You ask for Mees Jane?"

"Yes. Tell me, quick, do you know where she is?"

"Mees Jane mus' be at house," said Miguel, passing a hand over his eyes as if bewildered.

"She is not," said Rudolph. "She is gone, and both her nurses are gone."

"Inez gone?" repeated the old man, stupidly. "Ah; then she have carried away Mees Jane! I was 'fraid of that."

"Carried her away! Why should she do that?" asked Arthur impatiently.

"She jealous of New York girl—Mees Travers. Inez say she kill Mees Travers; but I tell her no. I say better not. But Inez hate thees girl for taking Mees Jane away from her. Inez love baby, Meest Weld; too much to be safe nurse."

While Arthur tried to comprehend this strange information Rudolph said to Miguel:

"Then you haven't seen the baby? You don't know where she is?"

The old Mexican gave him a keen look.

"No, Meest Hahn."

"You don't know where Inez has gone?"

"No, Meest Hahn."

"Nor the other nurse—the American girl?"

"No, Meest Hahn."

They hurried back to the house, leaving the old Mexican standing motionless beside the path.

CHAPTER VIII—VERY MYSTERIOUS

Arthur found Louise developing hysteria, while Beth, Patsy and Helen Hahn were working over her and striving to comfort her. Uncle John, the major and big Runyon stood gazing helplessly at the dolorous scene.

"Well? Well?" cried Mr. Merrick, as Weldon and young Hahn entered. "Any news?"

Arthur shook his head and went to his wife, bending over to kiss her forehead.

"Be brave, dear!" he whispered.

It needed but this tender admonition to send the young mother into new paroxysms.

"See here; we're wasting time," protested Runyon, his voice reaching high C in his excitement. "Something must be done!"

"Of course," cried Patsy, turning from Louise. "We're a lot of ninnies. Let us think what is best to do and map out a logical program."

The others looked at her appealingly, glad to have some one assume command but feeling themselves personally unequal to the task of thinking logically.

"First," said the girl, firmly, "let us face the facts. Baby Jane has mysteriously disappeared, and with her the two nurses."

"Not necessarily with her," objected Rudolph. "Let us say the two nurses have also disappeared. Now, the question is, why?"

A shriek from Louise emphasised the query.

"Don't let's bother with the 'why?'" retorted Patsy. "We don't care why. The vital question is 'where?' All we want, just now, is to find baby and get her back home again to her loving friends. She can't have been gone more than four hours—or five, at the most. Therefore she isn't so far away that an automobile can't overtake her."

"But she can't walk, you know," squeaked Runyon. "Baby didn't go alone; some one took her."

"True enough," observed Uncle John. "You're wrong, Patsy. We must try to decide who took baby, and why. Then we might undertake the search with a chance of success."

"Whoever took baby went on foot," persisted Miss Doyle. "The only four automobiles in the neighborhood are now standing in our driveway and in the garage. This is a country of great distances, and no matter in what direction the baby has been taken an auto is sure to overhaul her, if we don't waste valuable time in getting started."

"That's right!" cried Arthur, turning from Louise. "The theory agrees with old Miguel's suspicion about Inez, and—"

"What suspicion?" cried half a dozen.

"Never mind that," said Rudolph, with a hasty glance toward Louise; "let's be off, and talk afterward."

"We men must decide on our routes and all take the road at once," proposed Rudolph.

"It's pitch dark," said Runyon.

"Would you like to wait until morning?" demanded Rudolph, sarcastically.

"No; I want to rescue that baby," said the big fellow.

"Then take the north road, as far as Tungar's ranch. Stop at every house to inquire. When you get to Tungar's, come back by the McMillan road. That's a sixty mile jaunt, and it will cover the north and northwest. Take Mr. Merrick with you. Now, then, off you go!"

Runyon nodded and left the room, followed gladly by Uncle John, who longed to be doing something that would count. The others soon heard the roar of the motor car as it started away on its quest.

Then it was arranged for Arthur to drive back to Escondido to make inquiries and to watch the departure of the evening train, the only one to pass the station since baby had been missing. He was to carry Major Doyle with him and return by another route. Hahn promised to cover with his own car the only other two roads that remained to be searched, and he figured that they would all return to the house within two or three hours, when—if still there was no news—they might plan a further pursuit of the fugitive baby.

Helen Hahn had promised not to leave Louise until baby was found, and before starting Arthur assisted his wife to her room, where he left her weeping dismally one moment and screaming for little Jane the next.

Sing Fing had sent a maid to announce dinner, but no one paid any attention to the summons.

After the three automobiles had departed, Patsy and Beth remained in the nursery and left Helen and a maid with Louise. Once alone, Miss Doyle said to her cousin:

"Having started them upon the search, Beth, you and I must take up that pertinent suggestion made by Mr. Hahn and face the important question: 'Why?'"

"I'm dying to be of some use, dear," responded Beth in a disconsolate tone, "but I fear we two girls are quite helpless. How can *we* tell why the baby has been stolen?"

"Has she been stolen?" inquired Patsy. "We mustn't take even that for granted. Let us be sensible and try to marshal our wits. Here's the fact: baby's gone. Here's the problem: why?"

"We don't know," said Beth. "No one knows."

"Of course some one knows. Little Jane, as our friend Bul Run reminded us, can't walk. If she went away, she was carried. By whom? And why? And where?"

"Dear me!" cried Beth, despairingly; "if we knew all that, we could find baby."

"Exactly. So let's try to acquire the knowledge."

She went into Mildred's room and made an examination of its contents. The place seemed in its usual order, but many of Mildred's trinkets and personal possessions were scattered around.

"Her absence wasn't premeditated," decided Patsy. "Her white sweater is gone, but that is all. This fact, however, may prove that she expected to be out after dark. It is always chilly in this country after sundown and doubtless Mildred knew that."

"Why, she used to live here!" cried Beth. "Of course she knew."

Patsy sat down and looked at her cousin attentively.

"That is news to me," she said in a tone that indicated she had made a discovery. "Do you mean that Mildred once lived in this neighborhood?"

"Yes; very near here. She told me she had known this old house well years ago, when she was a girl. She used to visit it in company with her father, a friend of old Señor Cristoval."

"Huh!" exclaimed Patsy. "That's queer, Why didn't she tell us this, when we first proposed bringing her out here?"

"I don't know. I remember she was overjoyed when I first suggested her coming, but I supposed that was because she had at last found a paying job."

"When did she tell you of this?"

"Just lately."

"What else did she say?"

"Nothing more. I asked if she had any relatives or friends living here now, but she did not reply."

"Beth, I'm astonished!" asserted Patsy, with a grave face. "This complicates matters."

"I don't see why."

"Because, if Mildred knows this neighborhood, and wanted to steal baby and secrete her, she could take little Jane to her unknown friends and we could never discover her hiding-place."

"Why should Mildred Travers wish to steal baby?" asked Beth.

"For a reward—a ransom. She knows that Arthur Weldon is rich, and that Uncle John is richer, and she also knows that dear little Toodlums is the pride of all our hearts. If she demands a fortune for the return of baby, we will pay it at once."

"And prosecute her abductor, Mildred, afterward," said Beth. "No, Patsy; I don't believe she's that sort of a girl, at all."

"We know nothing of her history. She is secretive and reserved. Mildred's cold, hard eyes condemn her as one liable to do anything. And this was such an easy way for her to make a fortune."

Beth was about to protest this severe judgment, but on second thought remained silent. Appearances were certainly against Mildred Travers and Beth saw no reason to champion her, although she confessed to herself that she had liked the girl and been interested in helping her.

"We have still Inez to consider," said she. "What has become of the Mexican girl?"

"We are coming to her presently," replied Patsy. "Let us finish with Mildred first. A girl who has evidently had a past, which she guards jealously. A poor girl, whose profession scarcely earned her bread-and-butter before we engaged her. A girl whose eyes repel friendship; who has little to lose by kidnapping Jane in the attempt to secure a fortune. She was fond of baby; I could see that myself; so she won't injure our darling but will take good care of her until we pay the money, when Toodlums will be restored to us, smiling and crowing as usual. Beth, if this reasoning is correct, we needn't worry. By to-morrow morning Arthur will receive the demand for ransom, and he will lose no time in satisfying Mildred's cupidity."

"Very good reasoning," said Beth; "but I don't believe a word of it."

"I hope it is true," said Patsy, "for otherwise we are facing a still worse proposition."

"Inez?"

"Yes. Inez isn't clever; she doesn't care for money; she would not steal Jane for a ransom. But the Mexican girl worships baby in every fibre of her being. She would die for baby; she—" lowering her voice to a whisper, "she would *kill* anyone for baby."

Beth shivered involuntarily as Patsy uttered this horrible assertion.

"You mean—"

"Now, let us look at this matter calmly. Inez has, from the first, resented the employment of Mildred as chief nurse. She has hated Mildred with a deadly hatred and brooded over her fancied wrongs until she has lost all sense of reason. She feared that in the end baby Jane would be taken away from her, and this thought she could not bear. Therefore she has stolen baby and carried her away, so as to have the precious one always in her keeping."

"And Mildred?" asked Beth.

"Well, in regard to Mildred, there are two conjectures to consider. She may have discovered that Inez had stolen baby and is now following in pursuit. Or—"

"Or what, dear?" as imaginative Patsy hesitated, appalled by her own mental suggestion.

"Or in a fit of anger Inez murdered Mildred and hid her body. Then, to escape the penalty of her crime, she ran away and took baby with her. Either one of these suppositions would account for the absence of both nurses."

Beth looked at her cousin in amazement.

"I think," said she, "you'd better go and get something to eat; or a cup of tea, at least. This excitement is—is—making you daffy, Patsy dear."

"Pah! Food would disgust me. And I'm not crazy, Beth. Dreadful things happen in this world, at times, and Louise has a queer lot of people around her. Think a moment. Our baby has disappeared. Her two nurses, neither of whom are especially trustworthy, have also disappeared. There's a reason, Beth, and you may be sure it's not any common, ordinary reason, either. I'm trying to be logical in my deductions and to face the facts sensibly."

"Inez would be as careful of baby's welfare as would Mildred."

"I realize that. If I thought for a moment that baby was in any peril I would go distracted, and scream louder than poor Louise is doing. Do you hear her? Isn't it awful?"

"Let us tell Louise these things," said Beth, rising from her chair. "What you call your 'deductions' are terribly tragic, Patsy, but they reassure us about baby. Shall we go to Louise?"

"I think it will be better," decided Patsy, and they left the nursery and stepped out into the court. At the far end of the open space stood huddled a group of men, all of whom bore lanterns. Patsy advanced to the group and discovered them to be the Mexican laborers from the quarters. Old Miguel advanced a pace and bowed.

"We search for baby—for Mees Jane—eh?" he said, questioningly, as if desiring instructions.

"That is a happy thought, Miguel," replied the girl. "The others are scouring the roads in their motor cars, but the country needs searching, too—away from the roads, in the fields and orchards. Send your men out at once, and scatter them in all directions."

Miguel turned and rapidly harangued his followers in the Spanish patois.

One by one they turned and vanished into the night. Only the old man remained.

"Ever'bod' love Mees Jane," he said simply. "They all want to find her, an' ask me to let 'em go. Good. They will search well."

In spite of the words there was a tone of indifference in Miguel's voice that attracted the girl's notice. He did not seem in the least worried or agitated, nor did he appear to attach much importance to the search. Yet Patsy knew the aged foreman was one of "Mees Jane's" most devoted admirers.

"Where do you think baby is?" she asked abruptly.

"Quien sabe?" he answered, and then in English, "who knows?"

"Be sensible, Miguel! No one would hurt the dear child, I'm sure."

His dark features wrinkled in an engaging smile.

"No one would hurt Mees Jane. I believe it."

"But some one has carried her away."

He shrugged his shoulders.

"Some time she come back," said he.

"Now, see here, Miguel; you know more than anyone else about this affair. Tell me the truth."

He raised his brows, shaking his head.

"I know nothing," said he. "I not worry much; but I know nothing."

"Then you suspect."

The old man regarded her curiously; almost suspiciously, Patsy thought.

"What ees suspec'?" he asked. "It ees nothing. To suspec' ees not to know. Not to know ees—nothing at all."

The girl stamped her foot impatiently, for she caught Beth smiling at her.

"What is Inez to you, Miguel?" she demanded.

Again he smiled the childlike, engaging smile.

"She ees to me nothing," said he. "Inez is Mexican, but her family ees not my family. Not all Mexicans ees—re—spec'—ble. Once I know Inez' father. He drink too much wheesky, an' the wheesky make heem bad."

"But you like Inez?"

"She ees good to Mees Jane; but—she have bad tempers."

Patsy thought a moment.

"Did you know Mildred Travers when she used to live near here?" she asked.

Old Miguel started and took a step forward.

"Where she leeve, when she ees here?" he asked eagerly.

"I don't know. Have you ever seen her?"

"No. She do not come to our quarters."

"Wait a minute," said Patsy, and ran up to her room, leaving Beth to confront the ranchero and to study him with her dark, clear eyes. But she said nothing until her cousin returned and thrust a small kodak print into Miguel's hand.

"That is Mildred Travers," said Patsy.

Miguel held up his lantern while he examined the picture and both girls observed that his hand trembled. For a long time he remained bent over the print—an unnecessarily long time, indeed—but when he raised his head his face was impassive as a mask.

"I do not know Mees Travers," was all he said as he handed back the picture. "Now I go an' hunt for Mees Jane," he quickly added.

They watched him turn and noticed that his steps, as he left the court, were tottering and feeble.

"He lied," said Beth, softly.

60

"I am sure of it," agreed Patsy; "but that does not enlighten the mystery any. I'm sorry we brought Mildred to this place. There's just one thing you can bank on, Beth: that in some way or other Mildred is responsible for the disappearance of our precious Toodlums."

CHAPTER IX—A FRUITLESS SEARCH

Meantime, Uncle John and big Runyon were bowling along the north road, the lights gleaming from the powerful lanterns of the car and illuminating every object on either side of the way. The road seemed deserted and it was fully twenty minutes before they came to the first ranch house beyond that owned by Runyon himself. Here Mr. Merrick got out to make inquiries.

A tall, slovenly dressed woman answered his ring. She carried an oil lamp in her hand and eyed her late visitor severely.

"Have you seen a woman with a baby pass this way to-day—this afternoon?" asked the little man.

"Yes," was the reply; "she stopped here for supper."

Uncle John's heart gave a great bound.

"Have they gone on?" he inquired.

"Yes; an hour ago."

"Which way, ma'am?"

She nodded toward the north and Mr. Merrick hastily turned away. Then, pausing as a thought occurred to him, he asked:

"Was the—the baby—quite well, ma'am?"

"Seemed so," was the gruff answer and she slammed the door.

"Of course she was provoked," mused Uncle John, as he hurried back to the car. "I forgot to thank her. Never mind; we'll stop on our way back."

"Well?" demanded Runyon.

"We've got 'em!" was the joyful response. "They stopped here for supper and went on an hour ago. Drive ahead, and keep a sharp lookout."

"Who stopped here?" asked the other, as he started the car.

"Why the woman with the baby, of course."

"Which woman?"

"Which one? Oh, I didn't bother to ask. It doesn't matter, does it, whether it's Mildred or Inez. It's the baby we want."

Runyon drove on a while in silence.

"Did she describe little Jane accurately?" he asked, in his high, piping tenor.

"She didn't describe her at all," said Uncle John, provoked by such insistence. "There isn't likely to be more than one baby missing, in this lonely section of the country."

The big rancher made no reply. Both were keenly eyeing every object that fell under the light of the lamps. Presently they caught sight of a small white house half hidden by a grove of tall eucalyptus. There was no driveway, but the car was stopped at the nearest point and Uncle John got out. To his surprise Runyon followed him, saying:

"Two heads are better than one, sir."

"What do you mean by that, sir?" asked Mr. Merrick, sternly. "Don't you think I'm competent to ask a question?"

"You don't ask enough questions," returned Runyon frankly. "I'm not sure we're on the right trail."

"Well, I am," declared Uncle John, stiffly.

It took then some time to arouse the inhabitants of the house, who seemed to have retired for the night, although it was still early. Finally a woman thrust her head from an upper window.

"What's wanted?" she inquired in querulous tones.

"Have you seen a woman with a baby pass by here?" called Uncle John.

"No."

"Thank you, ma'am; sorry to have troubled you," said the little man, but in a very disappointed voice.

"Hold on a minute!" cried Runyon, as the woman was closing the window. "They told us at the last house that a woman with a baby stopped there for supper."

"Oh; they did, eh?"

"Yes; and she came in this direction; so we thought you might have seen her."

"Well, I might, if I'd looked in the glass," she said with grim humor. "I'm the woman."

"Oh, indeed!" cried Uncle John, feeling bewildered. "And the baby?"

"Safe asleep, if your yellin' don't wake him."

"Then—it's—*your* baby!"

"I'll swear to that. What do you want, anyhow?"

"We're looking for a lost baby," piped Bul Run.

"Then you'll hev to look somewhere else. I've walked all the way to town, an' back to-day, an' I'm dead tired. Are you goin' away, or not?"

They went away. Neither spoke as they again entered the car and started it upon the quest. Five minutes passed; ten; fifteen. Then Mr. Runyon said in a higher key than usual:

"There's nothing on a car as handy as a self-starter. All you have to do is —"

"Oh, shut up!" growled Uncle John.

They drove more slowly, after this, and maintained a sharp watch; but both men had abandoned all hope of discovering the missing baby on this route. When they reached Tungar's Ranch they crossed over to a less frequented road known as McMillan's which would lead them back to El Cajon, but by a roundabout, devious route.

The nearer they drew to the ranch the greater vigilance they displayed, but the road was deserted and no one at any of the ranch houses had seen or heard anything of a stray baby. As they turned into Arthur's driveway they overtook Rudolph Hahn, just returning from a quest as fruitless as their own. It was now half past nine o'clock.

Arthur Weldon and Major Doyle had both realized that the route awarded them was the most promising of all. It was scarcely conceivable that anyone who had stolen baby Jane would carry her farther into the unsettled districts. Far more likely that Toodlums' abductor would make for the nearest town or the railway station.

"If we know which one of the girls had taken baby," said Arthur, "we could figure better on what she would likely do. Inez would try to reach some Mexican settlement where she had friends, while Mildred might attempt to get into Los Angeles or San Diego, where she could safely hide."

"I can't believe either of them would steal little Jane," declared the major. "They are too fond of her for that."

"But the baby has been stolen, nevertheless," returned Arthur; "we can't get around that fact. And one of the nurses did it"

"Why?"

"Because the nurses disappeared with the baby."

"Then perhaps they've entered into a conspiracy, and both are equally guilty in the abduction," suggested the major.

"No; their hatred of one another would prevent any conspiracy between them. Only one stole the baby away, I'm quite sure."

"Then where's the other nurse?"

Arthur made no reply, but the major expected none. It was one of those mysteries that baffle the imagination. By and by Major Doyle made an attempt to answer his question himself, unconsciously using the same argument that his daughter Patsy had during her conversation with Beth.

"For the sake of argument, and to try to get somewhere near the truth," said he, "let us concede that, after we had gone to town, the two nurses quarreled. That would not be surprising; I've been expecting an open rupture between them. Following the quarrel, what happened? In view of the results, as we find them, two deductions are open to us. One girl may have made away with the other, in a fit of unreasoning rage, and then taken baby and run away to escape the consequences of her crime. If that conclusion is true, Inez is the more likely to be the criminal and it is Mildred's dead body we shall find in a clump of bushes or hidden in the cellar. That Mexican girl has a fierce temper; I've seen her eyes gleam like those of a wildcat as she watched Mildred kiss and cuddle little Jane. And she was so madly devoted to baby that she'd sooner die than part with her. Mildred is different; she's more civilized."

"To me, her eyes seem more treacherous than those of Inez," declared Arthur, who had liked the little Mexican nurse because she had been so fond of Toodlums. "They never meet your gaze frankly, those eyes, but seem always trying to cover some dark secret of which the girl is ashamed."

"Nevertheless, I maintain that she is the more civilized of the two," insisted the major. "She has a calmer, more deliberate nature. She wouldn't be likely to hurt Inez, while Inez would enjoy murdering Mildred."

"What's the other hypothesis?" asked Arthur.

"The more sensible one, by odds. After the quarrel, Inez grabs up baby and runs away, determined to escape from her hated rival and carry Jane beyond her influence. Soon after, Mildred discovers the flight of the Mexican and, impelled by her duty to you and her desire to circumvent Inez, rushes away in full chase, forgetting to leave any word. Perhaps she thought she would be able to return with baby before we arrived back from town; but Inez has led her a merry chase, which Mildred stubbornly refuses to abandon. I'm an old man, Arthur, and have seen a good deal of life, so mark my words: when the truth of this affair is known, it will be something like the story I've just outlined. I believe I've hit the nail on the head, and I'll admit it's bad enough, even that way."

"Then," said Arthur, more hopefully, "we may find Mildred and baby at home, when we return."

"Yes; and we may not. If they are home, Arthur, there are plenty there to look after the wee darling, and Louise will be comforted. On the other hand, if they don't return, it must be our business to find them. I can imagine Mildred, fagged out, in some far-away corner, resolving to stay the night and return to the ranch in the morning."

They remembered to have passed along this road before, that afternoon, on their way home from town. At that time they had seen no sign of the nurses or the baby. But to make assurance doubly sure Arthur stopped at every house to make inquiries and the road was inspected carefully. When they reached town they first visited the local police station and then the telephone office. Here they arranged to have every ranch house within a wide radius called and questioned in regard to the missing baby. Arthur also tried to get his own house, but the wire was still out of service.

Then to the telegraph office, where messages were sent to all the neighboring towns, giving descriptions of the missing baby and the nurses and offering a liberal reward for any news of their whereabouts.

By this time it was necessary to go to the depot, as the evening train was soon due. While they awaited its arrival Arthur and the major closely scanned every member of the group gathered at the station. Weldon even managed to have the train held, on its arrival, until he had passed through all the cars and assured himself that neither Mildred, Inez or baby Jane was aboard.

That automobile would have carried two despairing men away from the little town had it not been for the ray of hope suggested by the major that they would find baby safe at home on their arrival. However, that no chance might be neglected, they took another route, as originally arranged, and patiently continued their vain inquiries all the way back to the ranch. As they entered the driveway at El Cajon the clock in the brilliantly lighted hall of the mansion was striking ten.

Arthur rushed in and was met by Patsy.

"Any news?" they both cried eagerly; and then their expectant faces fell.

"How is Louise?" faltered Arthur.

"More quiet, now," answered the girl. "She became so violent, after you left, that we were all frightened; so Mrs. Hahn jumped into your little car and drove home, where she telephoned for the doctor. He happened to be at the Wilson place, so she caught him there and he came directly here. He is upstairs yet, but he gave Louise a quieting potion and I think she is now asleep."

Arthur started to mount the stairs; then hesitated.

"Are the boys back yet?" he asked.

"Yes; they are now out in the grounds, helping the Mexicans search the shrubbery."

The young man shuddered.

"I—I think I'll join them," he decided, and the major merely gave his daughter a solemn kiss and followed the bereaved father.

At the back of the mansion the lights of the lanterns were twinkling like fireflies, although the stars shone so brilliantly that all near-by objects were easily distinguished. Arthur and the major joined the men and for two hours longer the search was continued—more because they all felt they must be doing something, than through any hope of success.

Finally, at midnight, the chief searchers met in a group near the house, and Rudolph said: "Let's go in and rest a bit, and have a smoke. I'm about fagged out and, as a matter of fact, we've covered every inch of these grounds several times over."

Arthur silently turned and led the way into the house, where Patsy, Beth and Helen Hahn, all three worn and haggard, met them in the hall.

"Louise?" asked Arthur.

"Sleeping quietly," replied Beth. "Marcia is sitting beside her."

"Has Dr. Knox gone?"

"No; he's in the library, smoking. Eulalia is getting him something to eat, for it seems he missed his dinner."

"Why, so did I!" trilled big Runyon, in his clearest tenor. "I've just remembered it."

"You must all eat something," declared Patsy, "else you won't be fit to continue the search. Go to the library—all of you—and Beth and I will see what we can find in the kitchen."

CHAPTER X—CONJECTURES AND ABSURDITIES

In somber procession the men trailed up the stairs to the big library, where a dapper little man sat reading a book and puffing at a huge cigar. He looked up, as they entered, and nodded a head as guiltless of hair as was that of Uncle John. But his face was fresh and chubby, despite his fifty years, and the merry twinkle in his gray eyes seemed out of place, at first thought, in this house of anxiety and distress.

"Ah, Weldon; what news of little Jane?" he cheerfully inquired.

"None, Doctor."

"No trace at all?"

"None, whatever."

"That's good," declared the doctor, removing the ash from his cigar.

"Good!"

"Of course. No news is good news. I'll wager my new touring-car that our Jane is sound asleep and dreaming of the angels, this very minute."

"Has your new car a self-starter?" inquired Runyon anxiously, as if about to accept the wager.

"I wish I might share your belief, Doctor," said Arthur with a deep sigh. "It all seems a terrible mystery and I can think of no logical explanation to assure me of baby's safety."

"Yes, it's a mystery," agreed Dr. Knox. "But I've just thought of a solution."

"What is it?" cried half a dozen voices.

"Sit down and light up. I hope you all smoke? And you need

refreshment, for you've been working under a strain."

"Refreshments are coming presently," said Rudolph. "What's your solution, Doc?"

"The young ladies have been telling me every detail of the disappearance, as well as the events leading up to it. Now, it seems Mildred Travers is an old resident of this section of California. Was born here, in fact."

This was news to them all and the suggestion it conveyed caused them to regard Dr. Knox attentively.

"The old Travers Ranch is near San Feliz—about thirty miles south of here. I know that ranch by reputation, but I've never been there. Now for my solution. The Travers family, hearing that Mildred is at El Cajon, drive over here in their automobile and induce the girl to go home with them. She can't leave baby, so she takes little Jane along, and also Inez to help care for her. There's the fact, in a nutshell. See? It's all as plain as a pikestaff."

For a moment there was silence. Then big Runyon voiced the sentiment of the party in his high treble.

"You may be a good doctor," said he, "but you're a thunderin' bad detective."

"If I could telephone to the Travers Ranch, I'd convince you," asserted the doctor, unmoved by adverse criticism; "but your blamed old telephone is out of order."

"As for that," remarked Rudolph, taking a cigar from a box, "I've been a visitor at the Travers Ranch many times. Charlie Benton lives there. There hasn't been a Travers on the place since they sold it, ten or twelve years ago."

"Well," said the doctor, "I'm sorry to hear that. It was such a simple solution that I thought it must be right."

"It was, indeed, simple," admitted Runyon. "Ah! here comes food at last."

Patsy, Beth and Helen bore huge trays containing the principal dishes of the untasted dinner, supplemented with sandwiches and steaming coffee. This last the thoughtful Sing Fing had kept in readiness all the evening, knowing it would be required sooner or later.

Neither Uncle John nor the major was loth to partake of the much-needed refreshment. They even persuaded Arthur to take a cup of coffee. It was noticeable that now, whenever baby Jane was mentioned, they spoke her name in hushed whispers; yet no one could get away, for long, from the one enthralling subject of the little one's mysterious disappearance.

"What can we do now?" asked Arthur pleadingly. "I feel guilty to be sitting here in comfort while my darling may be suffering privations, or—or —"

"Really, there is nothing more to be done, just now," said Patsy, interrupting him before he could mention any other harrowing fears. "You have all done everything that mortals could do, for to-night, and in the morning we will resume the search along other lines. In my opinion you all ought to get to bed and try to rest, for to-morrow there will be a lot for you to do."

"What?" asked Arthur helplessly.

"Well, I think you ought to telegraph for detectives. If ever a mystery existed, here is one, and only a clever detective could know how to tackle such a problem."

"Also," added Beth, "you ought to telegraph to every place in California, ordering the arrest of the fugitives."

"I've done that already."

"Can't anyone think of a *reason* for the disappearance of these three persons—the baby and her two nurses?" inquired Mrs. Hahn earnestly. "It seems to me that if we knew what object they could have in disappearing, we would be able to guess where they've gone." Then the pretty little woman blushed at her temerity in making such a long speech. But the doctor supported her.

"Now that," said he, "strikes me as a sensible proposition. Give us the reason, some of you who know."

But no one knew a reason.

"Here are some facts, though," said Patsy. "Inez was baby's first nurse, and resented Mildred's coming. Somehow, I always get back to that fact when I begin to conjecture. The two nurses hated each other—everybody admits that. Mildred hated mildly; Inez venomously."

"Miguel told me that Inez has threatened to kill Mildred," said Arthur. "And there is another thing: one of the women said Inez brought the baby to the quarters, at about noon, and while there they discovered Mildred watching them from the shelter of a hedge. This incensed Inez and she hurried away to the house, followed stealthily by Mildred."

"That," said Dolph, "was perhaps the beginning of the quarrel. We don't know what happened afterward, except that both were seen in the court with baby at about two o'clock."

"Afterward," said Patsy, "one of the housemaids saw Inez go out—as if for a walk. She may have returned. I think she did, for otherwise it was Mildred who carried the baby away. I can see no reason for her doing that."

"Of course Inez returned," declared Arthur, "for nothing would induce her to run away from us and leave her beloved baby. I believe the poor girl would rather die than be separated for good from little Jane. You've no idea how passionately she worshiped the child."

"All of which," the doctor stated, "indicates a tragedy rather than some feminine whim—which last I much prefer as a solution. But if both nurses were fond of little Jane—who is the finest baby I ever knew, by the way—no quarrel or other escapade would permit them to injure the dear infant. Let us worry about the two girls, but not about little Jane."

Such advice was impossible to follow, and doubtless the shrewd doctor knew it; but it was a comforting thought, nevertheless, and had already done much to sustain the despairing father.

No one seemed willing to adopt Patsy's suggestion that they go to bed and get some much needed rest, in preparation for the morrow. Arthur left them for a time to visit Louise, but soon returned with word that she was quietly sleeping under the influence of the potion the doctor had administered. The three girls—for Mrs. Hahn was only a girl—sat huddled in one corner, whispering at times and trying to cheer one another. The doctor read in his book. Rudolph smoked and lay back in his chair, gazing reflectively at the ceiling. Bul Run had his feet on a second chair and soon fell into a doze, when he snored in such a high falsetto that Arthur kicked his shins to abate the nuisance. The major sat stiffly, gazing straight ahead, and Uncle John tramped up and down the room untiringly. The baby had grown very dear to the hearts of these last two men in the few days they had known her and her sudden loss rendered them inconsolable.

The suspense was dreadful. Had it been day, they could have done something to further the search, but the night held them impotent and they knew they must wear out the dreary hours as best they might.

At one o'clock Patsy drew her father aside and prevailed upon him to go to his room and lie down.

"This tedious waiting is merely wearing you out," she said, "and for dear baby's sake you should be fresh and vigorous in the morning."

That seemed to the major to be very sensible, especially as he felt the need of rest, so he slipped away and went to the blue room, which was located in the old wing and just above the nursery.

Then the girl approached Uncle John, but he would not listen to her. He was too nervous to rest, he insisted, and she realized that he spoke truly. Just as she abandoned the argument they were all startled by the sound of wheels rolling up the driveway and Arthur rushed to an open window and looked out.

An automobile had just arrived.

"Who is it?" he called.

"Id's me, Meisteh Veldon—id's Peters, de constable," called a rich voice in strong German dialect. "I got your baby here, und der Mexico girls to boots!"

"What!" they all shrieked, springing up to crowd around the window.

"Bring her in, Peters!" yelled Arthur, a great gladness in his voice, and now he was half running, half tumbling down the stairs in his haste to reach the door, while the others trailed after him like the tail of a comet.

As the door was thrown open Peters—a stout German—entered with a bundle in his arms, followed by a weeping, angry Mexican woman who was fat and forty and as unlike Inez as was possible.

Even as Arthur's eyes fell on this poor creature his heart sank, and the revulsion of feeling was so severe that he tottered and almost fell. Runyon grabbed his arm and supported him while Peters fumbled with the wrappings of the baby.

"Do I gets me dot rewards—heh?" asked the constable, holding up a fat little Mexican baby, whose full black eyes regarded the group wonderingly.

The father turned away, heartsick.

"Give him some money and get rid of him," he moaned.

Dolph took the constable in hand.

"You blooming idiot!" he exclaimed. "Why did you drag that poor woman here?"

"Id iss a rewards for der Mexico girl unt a baby; dot iss what ef'rybody say. How do I know id iss not Herr Veldon's baby?" demanded the indignant German. "Do his baby gots a sign on id, to say id iss de right baby, vot iss lost unt must be foundt? No, py jimminy! He yust say he hass a lost baby, unt a Mexico girl hass runned avay mit id. * * * So I finds me a Mexico girl unt a baby—unt here id iss!"

Patsy took the baby, a good little thing, and placed it in its mother's arms.

"Who are you, and where did this man find you?" the girl asked sympathetically.

The woman first shook her head and then burst into a voluble stream of Spanish, not a word of which could be understood.

"She cannot speak de Ingliss, like me, so I cannod tell if she iss de right Mexico vomans or nod," explained the constable. "Bud I brings her mit me, yust de same, unt id costs me four dollars to rendt me an automobubbles."

"Take her back," said Hahn, giving him a ten-dollar note; and then he gave the woman some money and kissed the baby, which smiled at him approvingly.

Beth ran to get some of the sandwiches for the woman, while Patsy brought milk for the baby and Uncle John offered the constable a cigar. Then the three were sent away and the automobile rolled back to town.

CHAPTER XI—THE MAJOR ENCOUNTERS THE GHOST

Ascending once more to the library the weary watchers resumed their former attitudes of waiting, as patiently as they might, for the coming of the day. Uncle John looked at his watch and found it was only a little after two o'clock. The minutes seemed hours to-night.

Suddenly a tremendous shriek rent the night, a shriek so wild and blood-curdling in its intensity that they sprang up and clung to each other in horror. While they stood motionless and terror-stricken there came a thump!—thump!—as of some heavy object tumbling down the three or four steps leading from the hall to the corridor of the old South Wing, and then the door burst open and Major Doyle—clothed in red-and-white striped pajamas—fairly fell into the library, rolled twice over and came to a stop in a sitting position, from whence he let out another yell that would have shamed a Cherokee Indian and which so startled big Runyon that he held a tenor note at high C for fully a minute—much like the whistle of a peanut roaster—the which was intended for an expression of unqualified terror.

Patsy was the first to recover and kneel beside the poor major, whose eyes were literally bulging from their sockets.

"Oh, Dad—dear Dad!—what is it?" she cried.

The major shuddered and clapped his hands to his eyes. Then he rocked back and forth, moaning dismally, while Patsy clung to his neck, sobbing and nearly distracted.

"Speak, Major!" commanded Arthur.

"A—a ghost!" was the wailing reply.

"A ghost!" echoed the amazed spectators.

"Did you *see* it?" questioned Uncle John in a trembling voice, as he bent over his brother-in-law.

"See it?" shouted the major, removing his hands to glare angrily at Mr. Merrick. "How could I see anything in the dark? The room was black as pitch."

"But you said a ghost."

"Of course I said a ghost," retorted the major, querulously, as he rubbed his bare ankle with one hand to soothe a bump. "You don't have to *see* a ghost to know it's there, do you? And this ghost—Oh, Patsy, darling, I can't say it! —it's too horrible."

Again a fit of shuddering seized him and he covered his eyes anew and rocked his body back and forth while he maintained his seat upon the floor. His legs were spread wide apart and he wiggled his big toes convulsively.

Beth asked with bated breath:

"Did you *hear* the ghost, then, Major?"

"Um! I heard it," he moaned. "And it's the end of all—the destroyer of our hopes—the harbinger of despair!"

"Look here, Major," said Uncle John desperately, "be a man, and tell us what you mean."

"It—it was baby—baby Jane!"

Arthur sobbed and dropped his head upon the table. Rudolph groaned. Runyon swore softly, but with an accent that did not seem very wicked. Uncle John stared hard at the major.

"You're an ass," he said. "You've had a nightmare."

The major could not bear such an aspersion, even under the trying circumstances. He scrambled to his feet, this time trembling with indignant anger, and roared:

"I tell you I heard baby—baby Jane—and she was crying! Don't I know?

Don't I know our baby's voice?"

Arthur leaped to his feet, a resolute expression upon his face. Instantly they all turned and followed him from the room. Into the hall, up the steps and through the corridor of the South Wing they passed, and just inside the major's room Rudolph struck a match and lighted a lamp that stood upon the table.

The place was in wild disorder, for when the major leaped from the bed he had dragged the coverings with him and they lay scattered upon the floor. The chair in which he had placed his clothing had been overturned and there was no question that his flight had been a precipitous rout. The casement of the window, set far back in the thick adobe wall, was wide open and the night breeze that came through it made the flame of the lamp flicker weirdly.

Beth proved her courage by bolding crossing the room and closing the window, while the others stood huddled just inside the door. Back of them all was the white face of Major Doyle, a brave soldier who had faced the enemy unflinchingly in many a hard fought battle, but a veritable poltroon in an imaginary ghostly presence.

Scarcely daring to breathe, they stood in tense attitudes listening for a repetition of the baby's cry. Only an awesome, sustained silence rewarded them.

The major's open watch upon the table ticked out the minutes—five—ten—fifteen. Then the doctor crept back to the library and quietly resumed his book. Presently Runyon joined him.

"Between you and me, Doc," said the big fellow, "I don't take much stock in ghosts."

"Nor I," returned Dr. Knox. "Major Doyle is overwrought. His imagination has played him a trick."

Rudolph Hahn entered and lighted a fresh cigar.

"Curious thing, wasn't it?" he said.

"No; mere hallucination," declared the doctor.

"I don't know about that," answered the boy. "Seems to me a ghost would do about as a person in life did. The child cried—poor little baby Jane! —and the ghostly wail was heard in the one room in this house that is haunted —the blue room. Perhaps there's something about the atmosphere of that room that enables those who have passed over to make themselves heard by us who are still in the flesh."

He was so earnest that the doctor glanced at him thoughtfully over the top of his book.

"It's the dead of night, and you're agitated and unreasonable, Hahn. In the morning you'll be ashamed of your credulity."

Dolph sat down without reply. His wife came in and sat beside him, taking his hand in hers. In another quarter of an hour back came Uncle John, shivering with the chill of the corridor, and stood warming himself before the grate fire.

"If the major heard the baby," he said reflectively, "it must be proof that —that something—has happened to the little dear, and—and we must face the worst."

"Well, it was baby I heard," asserted the major, who, having hastily donned his clothes, now made his reappearance in the library. "I was lying in a sort of dose when the cry first reached my ears. Then I sat up and listened, and heard it again distinctly, as if little Jane were only two feet away. Then— then—"

"Then you tested your lungs and made your escape," added the doctor drily.

"I admit it, sir!" said Major Doyle, haughtily. "Had it been anyone else who encountered the experience—even a pill peddler—he would have fainted."

In the blue room Patsy and Beth alone remained with Arthur Weldon.

Not a sound broke the stillness. When an hour had passed, Patsy said:

"Won't you go away, Arthur? Beth and I will watch."

He shook his head.

"You can do no good by staying in this awful place," pleaded the girl, speaking in a whisper.

"If she—if baby—should be heard again, I—I'd like to be here," he said pathetically.

Patsy knew he was suffering and the fact aroused her to action.

"Father isn't a coward," she remarked, "and either he heard the cry, or he dreamed it. In the latter case it amounts to nothing; but if Jane really cried out, that fact ought to give us an important clue."

He started at this suggestion, which the girl had uttered without thought, merely to reassure him. Yet now she started herself, struck by the peculiar significance of her random words.

"In what way, Patsy?" asked Beth, calmly.

That was the spur she needed. She glanced around the room a moment and then asked:

"Who built this wing, Arthur?"

"Cristoval, I suppose. I've heard it was the original dwelling," he replied. "The rest of the house was built at a much later date. Perhaps two generations labored in constructing the place. I do not know; but it is not important."

"Oh, yes it is!" cried Patsy with increasing ardor. "The rest of the house is like many other houses, but—these walls are six or eight feet in thickness."

"Adobe," said Arthur carelessly. "They built strongly in the mission days."

"Yet these can't be solid blocks," persisted the girl, rising to walk nervously back and forth before the walls. "There must be a space left inside.

And see! the major's bed stands close to the outer wall, which is the thickest of all."

He stared at her in amazement and then, realizing the meaning of her words, sprang to his feet. Beth was equally amazed and looked at her cousin in wonder.

"Oh, Patsy!" she exclaimed, "the baby hasn't been lost at all."

"Of course not," declared Patsy, her great eyes brilliant with inspiration. *"She's imprisoned!"*

CHAPTER XII—ANOTHER DISAPPEARANCE

For a time the three stood regarding one another with startled eyes. Then Arthur gasped: "Great heaven! what fools we've been."

"Come!" cried Patsy. "The nursery."

They rushed down the corridors to the staircase and thence into the court. The door of the nursery stood ajar and Arthur first entered and lighted a lamp.

The light fell full upon the face of a man seated in a low rocking chair and holding a half smoked cigarette in his mouth. He was fast asleep. It was old Miguel, the ranchero.

Arthur shook his shoulder, savagely, and the man wakened and rubbed his eyes. Then, seeing who had disturbed him, he quickly rose and made his characteristic low, sweeping bow.

"What are you doing here?" demanded Weldon, angry and suspicious.

"I am look for Mees Jane," returned the old man calmly.

"In your sleep? Come, get out of here."

"Wait a minute, Arthur," said Beth, reading Miguel's face. "He knows something."

Arthur looked at the man critically, reflecting that there must be a reason for his presence in the nursery. Miguel had been fond of baby Jane. Was he merely disconsolate over her loss, or—did he really "know something"?

"Miguel once told me," said Patsy, speaking slowly, "that he used to live in this house, in Cristoval's time, and knows it thoroughly."

The old man bowed.

"I theenk," said he, "perhaps we find Mees Jane here—not somewhere else."

"Why do you think that, Miguel?"

It was Patsy who questioned him. He mused a bit before replying.

"The old señor—the father of my Señor Cristoval—was strange mans," said he. "He make thees house a funny way. Come; I show you."

He led the way to the little room adjoining, the one Inez had occupied. In one corner of the floor was a square hole, with steps leading down to a sort of blind pocket. Holding a lamp in one hand Miguel descended the steps and pushed against a block of adobe that formed part of the outer wall. It swung inward, disclosing a cavity about four feet in width and fully six feet high. The interior could be plainly seen from the room, by stooping close to the floor. There were shelves in the cavity and upon one of them stood a jar of milk.

"Oh," cried Patsy, clasping her hands together. "I told you the wall was hollow!"

Arthur followed Miguel down the steps. He took the lamp and examined the little room. All the walls that formed it seemed solid.

Miguel was holding the block that served as a door. He released his hold, when Arthur had again ascended, and the block swung back into place.

As they returned to the nursery, Weldon asked:

"Do you know of any other rooms in the wall, Miguel?"

The man shook his head, uncertainly.

"I know there be other rooms in thees wall," said he, "for Señor Cristoval have told me so. Hees father make the places to keep things safe from robbers—perhaps to hide from others, too. But where such places are ees the secret of the Cristovals. The room I show you ees all I know about. I thought that was secret, too; but no; the New York nurse tell Inez of that room, an' Inez she keep Mees Jane's milk there, to be cool."

"Mildred told of the room!" exclaimed Arthur in astonishment.

"Yes," said Beth, "she used to visit this house as a girl, when Cristoval lived here, and she must have known some of the secret rooms."

"Ah, that ees what I theenk," agreed old Miguel. "There ees more room in thees wall; that I know. If thees Mildreed know one room, she may know more. So I theenk she and Inez have go into some room of the wall an' take Mees Jane with them. Some way, they cannot get out again."

"Exactly!" cried Patsy triumphantly. "They are somewhere in that wall, imprisoned, and the major really heard the baby cry."

"But—Miguel, Miguel!" pleaded Arthur, earnestly, "can't you remember how the wall opens? Think! Think carefully."

"I do theenk, Meest Weld; I theenk till I go sleep, an' you find me here."

"Now, let's do some thinking ourselves," suggested Beth. "The opening that leads into the wall must be from this very room. Miguel thinks so, too, and that's why he came here. Let us examine the wall."

They undertook to do this, holding the lamps close to the adobe blocks and inspecting every crack. The cement used in joining the blocks had crumbled away at the outer edges in almost every instance, and it was impossible to tell if any block was removable or not. Miguel or Arthur pushed hard against every block in the room, from those nearest the floor to those far above their heads; but not one yielded a hair's breadth.

"Suppose we go outside," said Patsy. "Perhaps there is some window, or grating, that will give us a clue."

So they took old Miguel's lantern and went into the garden where they could view the outer side of the wall. A tangle of climbing vines grew against the wing, but there was no window or other opening on the first floor. Above, on the second floor, were two windows, one of which admitted light and air to the blue room.

"How about the other window?" asked Beth.

"That," said Arthur, "must be in an unused room at the end of the corridor. We have never furnished it."

"I think it might be well to examine that room," suggested Patsy.

So they reentered the house and, followed by Miguel, ascended to the second floor. The door of the library was ajar and those seated there, seeing Arthur and the girls pass, came trooping out to ask what they were doing.

Patsy briefly explained the new theory they had conceived to account for the disappearance of baby and the two nurses, and the idea was so startling that all became eager to join in the investigation.

They invaded the vacant room in a body, several of the men carrying lamps. It was in size and shape a duplicate of the blue room, with its one window deeply embedded in the wall, the surface of the embrasure being covered with heavy redwood planks.

From the fact that this room lay directly over the small one occupied by Inez, in which was the wall cavity they had recently explored, they conceived the idea that the wall here might also be hollow. Pounding upon it, however, had no effect in determining this, for kiln-baked adobe is not resonant and it was impossible to discover from any surface indication whether there were eight feet of closely set blocks or less. Careful search for any sign of an opening proved futile.

Finally old Miguel said:

"Next room was room of Señor Cristoval. Eet was room hees father live in, too; the old señor who build thees part of house. If there ees way to get in wall, from upstairs, it ees there."

"To be sure," said practical Beth, catching at the suggestion; "it was there that Major Doyle heard the baby cry."

So on they all trooped into the blue room, where the wall was likewise carefully inspected. While this was being done Rudolph looked at his watch and found it was after four o'clock.

"It will soon be daylight," said he to his wife. "What a night it has been!

It seems a month since we arrived here and found Toodlums gone."

Old Miguel had been silent and unobtrusive in the vacant room, but here he was as eager in testing the wall as any one of them.

"You see, it's this way," Patsy was saying; "if the major could hear baby cry, through this wall, those inside could hear us, if we called to them. Who among us has the clearest, the most penetrating voice?"

"Suppose *I* try?" squeaked Runyon, earnestly; but those who considered the remark at all merely gave him scornful looks.

"Let Rudolph call," said Helen. "I think his voice might penetrate the pyramids of Egypt."

Rudolph went close to the wall and shouted:

"Hello, there! Baby! I-nez!—eh—eh—what's the other girl's name?"

"Mildred," said Beth.

"Mil-dred!" shouted Dolph; "Mil-dred!"

He paused between each name, which he roared so loudly that he nearly deafened those in the room, and everyone listened intently for a response.

No answer.

"Perhaps they're asleep—worn out," said Uncle John. No one now seemed to doubt that the missing ones were imprisoned in the wall.

"Let Beth try," suggested Patsy.

Beth had a clear, bell-like voice and from where she stood she called out the names of Inez and Mildred. Then, in the stillness that followed, came a muffled cry in return—a cry that set all their nerves quivering with excitement.

The mystery was solved at last.

Beth repeated the call and now the answer was clearer, though still indistinguishable. It was a voice, indeed, but whose voice they could not tell.

But now, to their astonishment, came another sound, quite clear and distinct—
the wail of a baby voice.

"That settles it!" cried the major, triumphantly. "Was I right, or wrong?
Was it a nightmare, or was I crazy?"

"Neither one, my dear sir," replied the doctor. "You declared you heard a
ghost."

Arthur was capering about in frantic joy.

"She's alive—my baby is alive!" he exclaimed.

"And probably she was sound asleep until your infernal yelling
awakened her," added the major.

"It wasn't *our* yelling," said Uncle John, as delighted as even the father
could be; "it was the yelling of whoever is inside, there, that frightened the
baby. Thank goodness the dear child could sleep during all these weary hours,
when we have been wearing our hearts out with anxiety."

"We have yet cause for anxiety," declared Patsy, "for little Jane is not
rescued yet, by any means, and presently the poor thing will become very
hungry and suffer for lack of food. We now know where baby is, but we can't
get at her; nor can Mildred or Inez find a way to get her out, or they would
have done so long ago."

"Very true," agreed Helen Hahn, gravely. "Unless we can soon find a
way to get to them, all three will starve."

"Why, we will pull down the wall!" cried Arthur.

"Dynamite it!" piped Bul Run.

"Be sensible!" counseled Uncle John sternly. "We are wasting precious
time. Miguel," turning to the ranchero, "get some of your men, with picks and
crowbars, and fetch them here quickly."

The Mexican, who seemed bewildered by the discovery of the missing
ones, although he had himself been the first to suspect where they were,

started at once to obey this order. When he had gone, Patsy said:

"Of course there is some easy way to get inside the wall, and to get out again. Are we so stupid that none of us can penetrate the secret of the cunning Spaniard who built this place?"

The challenge merely led them to regard one another with perplexed looks.

"The fact that they're alive, after all these hours," said young Hahn, "is proof that they are supplied with air, and plenty of it. Then there is an opening, somewhere or other."

"Also," added Arthur, reflectively, "they are now opposite the second story rooms, when they must have entered the hollow wall at the first floor—perhaps from the nursery. That proves there is a stairway, or at least a ladder, inside."

At this moment a maid entered to say that Mrs. Weldon had awakened and was calling hysterically for her baby. The doctor and Patsy at once hurried to Louise's bedside, where the girl said:

"Don't worry, dear. Little Jane has been found and is now in this very house. So try to be quiet and go to sleep again."

"Bring her to me; bring my darling at once!" begged Louise. But the doctor now interfered.

"I don't wish to disturb baby at present," he said positively. "I think the child is sleeping. You have been quite ill, Mrs. Weldon, and I must insist on your remaining quiet. Here; drink this, if you please."

Louise, reassured, drank the potion and presently sank into another doze. Dr. Knox remained beside her for a time but Patsy hurried back to the blue room, eager to assist in the rescue of the prisoners.

"I'm afraid we're a stupid lot," Uncle John was saying as she entered; "or else the Spanish don was remarkably clever. We know the wall is hollow, and we know there's an opening, yet we can't solve the riddle."

But here came Miguel and two strong men laden with steel bars, cold chisels and picks. For a time it was a quandary where to attack the wall, but Arthur finally chose the place just back of the bed and bade the men begin their work.

The adobe proved harder than the hardest brick. Old Miguel knew that it must be broken away bit by bit, for he was not unacquainted with the material, yet even under his skillful direction the work progressed with aggravating slowness.

Daylight gradually crept into the room and rendered lamps unnecessary. The morning discovered a very disheveled, heavy-eyed group, not a single member of which was willing to retire from the fascinating scene of rescue.

Patsy went away to arouse Sing Fing and the servants, some of whom she found had remained awake all night. In half an hour steaming hot coffee was brought to the blue room and gratefully consumed by the weary watchers. Breakfast of a substantial character would soon be ready and it was agreed that part of them should eat at one time while the others remained to watch and to call them promptly if anything new developed.

Arthur, too nervous to stand idly by, insisted on attacking the wall in another place and Runyon assisted him, the latter's strength and muscle winning the admiration of all observers. He worked fiercely for a time, driving in the bar with stalwart blows and chipping off huge pieces of adobe. Then, dripping with perspiration, he retired in favor of Arthur and rested by taking a seat in the window, where the cool morning air could fan him.

Patsy noticed Runyon in this position, his back against the redwood planks and his legs stretched out on the window-seat; but the work on the wall drew her attention, as it did that of everyone else.

Suddenly there was a crash and a loud report—followed by a shrill cry— and as every eye turned to the window they found that Runyon's great body had absolutely disappeared. A rush was made to the window, but he did not seem to have fallen out. There was no sign of him at all. As if by magic, he was gone.

While they stood amazed and half frightened by the marvel of the thing, Patsy recovered sufficiently to say:

"Quick—let us get below! He must be under those rose vines, perhaps crushed and badly hurt."

So they made for the door and flocked downstairs and out into the garden. The vines seemed undisturbed. When the men pushed them aside there was no evidence of the big rancher to be seen. In fact, they were all convinced that Runyon had not fallen out of the window.

Slowly they returned to the blue room, where the major exclaimed, with positive emphasis:

"This room is haunted. Don't talk to me! There's no other explanation. If we don't watch out, we'll all disappear—and that'll be the end of us!"

CHAPTER XIII—THE WAY IT HAPPENED

Through consideration for the nerves and perhaps the credulity of the reader, it may be advisable at this juncture to go a little back in our story and relate the circumstances which led to the present perplexing crisis. A great detective once said that "every mystery has a simple solution"—meaning, of course, that the solution is simple when once discovered. Therefore, the puzzling mystery of the disappearance of baby Jane and her two nurses, followed later by the vanishment of Mr. Bulwer Runyon, was due to the one-time idiosyncracy of a certain Señor Cristoval, happily deceased, rather than to any supernatural agency.

Until now we have only known Mildred Travers, as she called herself, in a casual way. We know that she was considered a competent nurse and had proved her capability in the care of baby Jane. Also we know that she was silent and reserved and that her eyes bore an habitual expression that was hard and repellent. Without being able to find any especial fault with the girl, no one was attracted toward her—always excepting the baby, who could not be expected to show discrimination at her tender age.

A little of Mildred's former history had escaped her, but not enough to judge her by. She had once lived in Southern California, near this very place. She had visited this house frequently with her father, when a small child, and old Señor Cristoval had confided to her some of the secrets of the mansion. That was all. What had become of friends and family, how she went to New York and studied nursing, or what might account for that hard look in her eyes, no one now acquainted with her knew.

The Mexican girl, Inez, was nearly as peculiar and unaccountable as Mildred. There was no mystery about her, however, except that she was so capable and intelligent, considering her antecedents. Inez' people lived in a small town in another part of the county and the girl was one of a numerous brood of children whose parents were indolent, dissipated and steeped in ignorance. When fourteen years old she had left home to work for some of the neighboring ranchers, never staying in one place long but generally liked by her employers. The woman who had recommended Inez to Mrs. Weldon said she was bright and willing and more intelligent than most Mexicans of her class, but that she possessed a violent temper.

Louise had seen little evidence of that temper, however, for Inez from the first loved her new mistress and idolized the baby. It was only after Mildred came to supplant her, as she thought, that the girl developed an unreasoning, passionate hatred for the other nurse and was jealous of every attention Mildred lavished upon the little one.

The baby was impartial. She laughed and held out her chubby fists to either nurse, perhaps realizing that both were kind to her. It was this that made Inez so furious and caused Mildred to disdain the Mexican girl. The two were at sword's points from the first, although after a little Mildred made an attempt to conciliate Inez, knowing that the untutored Mexican was by nature irresponsible and jealous, but withal loving and generous.

Inez did not respond to these advances, but as the days passed she became less sullen when in the presence of Mildred, and at times, when busied over her duties, so far forgot her animosity as to converse with her in her old careless, unaffected way. Only Mildred was able to note this slight change, and it encouraged her to believe she might win Inez' confidence in the end. Inez herself did not realize that she had changed toward the "witch-woman," and when brooding over her fancied wrongs hated Mildred as cordially as ever.

On the day when the Weldons and their guests rode into town, the two nurses had indulged in a longer and more friendly conversation than usual. It began by Mildred's chiding the Mexican for taking baby to the quarters unknown to her, as she had been obliged to follow to see what had become of the child. Inez retorted by accusing Mildred of spying upon her. Their return to the house was anything but friendly, and Inez flatly refused to obey such instructions as Mildred gave her for the care of baby. She even walked out of the court in a temper and was gone for an hour. Then she stole in, a little ashamed of her revolt, but still defiant and rebellious.

They were in the nursery and Mildred pretended not to notice her assistant's mood.

"I have prepared two bottles of baby's food," said she. "Please place one in the hollow of the wall, in your room, to keep cool until we need it."

"I won't!" said Inez.

"Why not?" asked Mildred quietly.

"Because you are witch-woman," cried the Mexican; "because you use bad magic to make hollow in wall; because you try to make baby witch-woman, like yourself, by keeping her milk in the witch-place; because—because—I *hate* you!" she concluded with a passionate stamp of her foot.

Mildred looked upon the girl pityingly as she crossed herself again and again as if in defiance of the supposed witchcraft. The poor girl sought by this method to ward off any evil charm Mildred might attempt in retaliation, and the action nettled the trained nurse because the unjust accusation was so sincerely made.

She slowly rose and taking the bottle of milk carried it herself to the hollow in the wall and placed it upon a shelf. Then, returning, she stood before the petulant, crouching Mexican and said gently:

"Were I truly a witch, Inez, I would not be working as a nurse—just as you are. Nor do I know any magic, more than you yourself know."

"Then how you know about that hole in the wall?" demanded Inez.

"I wish you would let me explain that. Indeed, I think a good talk together will do us both good. Take this chair beside me, and try to believe in my good will. I do not hate you, Inez. I wish you did not hate me."

Inez slowly rose from the floor and seated herself in the chair, turning it so that she could eye Mildred's face as she spoke.

"When I was a girl," continued Mildred, "I often came to this house to visit. Sometimes I stayed here for several days, while my father talked with his old friend, old Señor Cristoval."

"That is a lie," asserted Inez. "I have ask Miguel, who is here forty years, an' was house servant for Señor Cristoval. Miguel say there is no Señor Travers who is friend of Señor Cristoval. No Señor Travers did ever come to this house for visit. What you say to that, Witch-Woman?"

Mildred flushed and seemed embarrassed. Then she answered calmly:

"I think Miguel speaks truly, for my father did not bear the name of Travers. He was called by another name."

"Then why do you call yourself Travers?" retorted the other.

Mildred hesitated.

"I did not like my old name," she said, "and so I changed it. But this is a secret I have told you, Inez, and you must not tell anyone of it."

Inez nodded, looking at the other curiously. This confession had aroused her sympathy, for the first time, for her fellow nurse. The fact that there was a secret between them dissolved to an extent her antipathy for Mildred, and it might be a bond to eventually draw them nearer together. With more tolerance than she had yet shown she asked:

"Did Señor Cristoval show you the secrets of this house?"

"Yes. I was a little girl and he was good to me. I am not a witch-woman, Inez. Oh, if I were, I would witch a little happiness into my life!" she added miserably.

This burst of rebellious longing interested Inez even more than the secret. She could understand such a protest against fate.

"At first," continued Mildred, reverting to her former cold speech, while the hard look, which for an instant had given way to a flash of sentiment, again crept into her eyes, "I thought I had forgotten the queer recesses and secret rooms built by the elder Cristoval; but now I am beginning to remember them. In the days when this wing was built, the country was wild and lawless. Robbers often visited a house in broad daylight and took away all that was of value; so the first Cristoval—the father of the one I knew—made the secret place to hide his treasure in, and even to hide himself and his family if the thieves threatened them."

"Is the treasure there now?" asked Inez eagerly.

Mildred frowned, as if the question displeased her.

"Of course not. That was long ago. When I was a girl they no longer needed the rooms in the wall as a hiding-place from thieves; but they kept them secret, just the same. I think I am the only person Señor Cristoval ever told. He did it to please me, I suppose, because I was a child."

Inez was much impressed. She began to regard Mildred more amicably. If she were not a witch-woman, she reflected, there was no reason to fear her. The Mexican girl thought deeply on what she had heard, during the next half hour. She watched Mildred put the baby to sleep and then take up a book to read as she sat beside the crib. Inez went out into the deserted court and squatting beside the fountain pondered upon the fascinating mysteries of the old house.

She crept back, presently, and reentered the nursery where Mildred was sitting.

"Tell me," she began, in a friendly and familiar way that was new in her relations with the other girl, "are there indeed rooms hidden in these walls—big enough for people to hide in?"

Mildred smiled and laid down her book. Inez in this mood was worth cultivating, if she hoped to win her confidence. It would be far easier to get on in her new situation if Inez would learn to like her.

Another thing influenced her: a reflection that had not been absent from her mind since the Weldons departed for the day and had left her practically in charge of the house. She had come to this house for a purpose. Could that purpose be best accomplished to-day, or at some later period?

"I believe," she answered musingly, "that this wall back of us is hollow and contains several rooms, which may be entered at various secret places—if one knows where the places are."

"They cannot be very big rooms," said Inez in a hushed, awed voice, as she glanced at the wall.

"No; they must be narrow. But they are quite long and high—some of them—and there are stairs leading from one floor to another, just like the big stairs in the hall."

Inez stared at her.

"How you know that?" she inquired.

"Why, I've seen the rooms," was the reply. "Let me think a moment."

During the pause she scrutinized the Mexican girl closely, wondering if it would be advisable to take her into her confidence. Then she continued, speaking slowly:

"I'm almost sure it was in this very room that one of the secret entrances was built. It was not a nursery when I was here before, you know; it was Señor Cristoval's office, where he kept his books and his money-boxes."

She rose, as she spoke, and looked uncertainly up and down the wall. Then, with a nod of satisfaction, she quickly walked to the east corner and counted four blocks of adobe, starting from the floor. The fourth line of blocks she followed to the third one, and placed her hand upon it.

"I think I am right, so far," she said. "This is the door to the secret rooms, but the key that unlocks it is somewhere in the floor. Turn back the rug, please, Inez."

The girl obeyed, her brown fingers trembling with excitement. The floor was of adobe blocks similar to those which formed the wall, but smaller in size. Mildred regarded them reflectively and then placed her foot on the edge of the second block directly in a line with the place where her hand rested. The pressure of her foot made the block tip slightly, and observing this she pressed hard with her hand against the inner edge of the upper block.

The result seemed magical. Three seemingly solid blocks of the wall swung slowly outward, disclosing a dimly lighted recess beyond.

Mildred stepped in, stooping her head slightly because the opening was so small. Inez followed her, nervously seizing the other girl's hand for support. The light seemed to come from some place far above and as their eyes grew accustomed to it they could discern a passage about three feet in width and fourteen feet long, which occupied the center of the wall. At the right, a flight of steps led upward, and to their left the place was occupied by some chairs and stools. Against the walls were several narrow shelves, easily reached by one standing upright.

"Why, they have left the place furnished, just as it was when Señor Cristoval first showed it to me," said Mildred. "The mattings and upholstery must be ready to fall to pieces, by this time; but you see, Inez, I was right about the secret rooms."

Just then little Jane wakened with a lusty cry.

"See to the baby," said Mildred quickly, and the Mexican girl reluctantly turned away to obey.

Mildred remained in the recess, thoughtfully eyeing the various antique objects which had been allowed to remain there, some of which were of real value. She reflected that the last Cristoval had doubtless passed away without disclosing the secret of the wall to anyone, and his executors, in selling the mansion, had been quite unaware that anything was hidden in the adobe wall. Without doubt the property might now be justly claimed by the new owner, Arthur Weldon, and this thought made Mildred flush with eager resolve to take full advantage of her present opportunity. For here was the consummation of her hopes; here was the realization of the important plan which had brought her to Southern California and to this house.

Inez had caught the baby from its cradle and, holding a bottle of fresh milk-food to its lips to comfort it, again advanced through the opening. Mildred had stepped a few paces along the passage and Inez, the baby in her arms, started to join her.

At that moment she heard a sound in the court, as of some one approaching, and to avoid letting others know of this fascinating secret the girl thoughtlessly grasped the adobe door with her free hand and swung it shut behind her.

It closed with a sharp "click!" and Mildred, hearing the sound, turned with a low cry of fear.

"Great heavens, what have you done?" she exclaimed in tense tones and brushing the Mexican aside she threw her whole weight against the wall. It did not yield a hair's breadth.

Inez, with terror in her eyes, stared at her companion.

"Is it lock?" she whispered.

Mildred pushed again, straining every muscle. Then she bent and examined the wall. It was easy to see, from this side, where the series of three blocks were firmly joined together. Also the butts of three huge iron hinges protruded slightly into the passage. There could be no mistake. The closing of the door had made them prisoners.

CHAPTER XIV—PRISONERS OF THE WALL

Mildred silently turned and regarded her companion. Her eyes were not hard and cold now. They were glowing with anxiety and terror.

"Cannot we get out?" demanded Inez.

Mildred shook her head.

"Not the way we came in," she replied. "I remember now that Cristoval warned me never to close the door behind me; but I forgot to tell you that, so you are not to blame."

Inez looked down at baby, who had again fallen asleep, snuggled close to her breast. Her fear at this time was not for herself. It was dreadful to think of the danger she had placed the darling baby in—the child she would have died rather than injure.

Mildred saw the look and read its anguish. Her own cheeks blanched for a moment, but there was an inherent quality of courage in this girl that forbade her to despair. Speaking as much to herself as to Inez she said:

"We were able to open this adobe door only by pressing downward on a block of the floor outside, which released a catch which is securely hidden in the lower edge of the opening—where I cannot reach it. So, unless some one knew the secret and could press that block in the nursery, the door cannot again be opened."

Inez staggered to a stool and sat down.

"Must we stay here always?" she pleaded piteously.

"I think not. I am *sure* not, Inez. They will find some way to break through the wall and rescue us."

"But no one knows we are here!"

"True. Well, I believe there are other ways to get out of this hollow wall, besides the opening we came through. I am quite certain I was told that Señor Cristoval could enter from his room, on the second floor; and perhaps there are other entrances. Stay here and keep baby quiet and I will make an examination of our prison."

As she started to ascend the stairs Inez arose to follow her.

"Let me come, too," she begged. "I am afraid to stay alone."

"Very well; but try not to waken baby."

The stairs were built the full width of the space, completely blocking it at that end. At the top they stepped into another narrow room, which was not over the lower one but extended farther along the wall. It was, indeed, extraordinary to note how comfortable the genius of that ancient Cristoval who had planned the place, had made this originally comfortless corridor-like room, for room it was despite its narrow confines.

The ceiling was high, and light and air were admitted by gratings placed at the top, letting onto the bastion of the roof, where they could not be observed by those below. The gratings were covered by projections that kept out the rain and dew. On the floor was a thick carpet, somewhat musty and dusty now, and at the far end was placed a couch with silken curtains. This was still piled high with bedding and pillows and was boxed in, the full width of the passage, with elaborately carved woods. Upholstered seats, rather narrow but long and quite comfortable, were built against the wall and supported by richly carved frames of ebony and panels of cherry. There were pictures upon the walls; oil paintings of quite good quality. A sort of wall-cabinet and some small brackets supported numerous hooks, ornaments, and several boxes of metal and sandalwood, which last Mildred eyed expectantly but had now no leisure to examine.

The girls were both awed by this discovery, for Mildred had never been permitted to mount the stair to this room when Señor Cristoval had allowed her to peep into the lower passage. The intense silence lent a weirdness to the place that was at first quite disconcerting. A gray rat scuttled along the carpet, causing them to jump and cry out, and then disappeared somewhere beneath the couch. Inez, trembling with nervous fear, hugged the baby with one arm and clutched Mildred's arm with the other, and then they sat together on one of the cushioned seats and tried to collect their thoughts.

Mildred reflected that no person had entered this place for at least eight years, for it was eight years since the last Cristoval had passed to his fathers. Yet, aside from the dust, everything seemed in an excellent state of preservation. The secret room had been fitted up by its builder more than fifty years before and much of the furnishings must have been placed there then.

"My first task," she said to Inez, "must be to make a thorough examination of this place. Since there is no one to help us, we must help ourselves, and any weakness at this time would be fatal."

With this she rose and carefully began to inspect the walls. The heavy carpet was merely laid flat on the adobe floor and she raised it here and there and tested the blocks to see if any was movable. There was no means of reaching the ceiling but an opening there was out of the question.

Near the center of the room, on the inner wall and about two feet from the floor, was a square of wood firmly embedded in the adobe. This, she thought, might possibly be a means of egress or ingress, so she tested it eagerly, pressing not only upon the wood but on all the blocks of adobe near it, in the endeavor to discover a hidden spring or some other clever mechanical contrivance which would prove the "open sesame." But the panel and the wall defied all her efforts and she finally concluded it was solid planking placed there to support the wall or to allow cupboards or shelves to be nailed against it.

Another similar place, where a huge panel of plank was set in the wall, she found at the very end of the passage, beyond the couch, and was only able to reach it by mounting the bed and climbing over the bedding. This panel was also immovable and she decided it could not be an opening because the wall beyond it was doubtless solid. This space beyond the bed, where the room ended, contained a huge chest of quaintly carved oak. As she saw the chest her heart gave a great bound and forgetting for the moment her desire to escape she reached down and raised the lid.

Then her face fell. Despite the dim light in this corner, which she had grown somewhat accustomed to in investigating the panel, she could see that the chest contained merely papers, with which it was half filled. This might be the accumulated correspondence of the Cristovals, of no use to any but themselves, and losing all interest in the chest she closed the lid and again crossed over the high bed to Inez.

The result of this investigation, which had consumed a full hour, so thorough had she been, convinced Mildred that there was no immediate way for them to leave their prison. So she began to plan how they might keep themselves and baby Jane comfortable until they were rescued.

The bottle of milk, which Inez still held in her hand, was a prepared food of a highly nourishing quality. The contents of the bottle had scarcely been touched by baby when, rousing from her sleep, she had been taken up and comforted by Inez until slumber again overtook her. Usually Jane consumed two bottles of such food each day, and another during each night.

Mildred looked at her watch and found it was nearly four o'clock. With a little care in its administration the baby's food might last until morning, but not longer. For themselves, they must be content without food, unless—

She decided to search the boxes and shelves while daylight lasted, and bade Inez place the sleeping infant on one of the cushioned seats and support it with a pillow brought from the couch. Then the two girls began to take down the boxes from the shelves and explore their contents. Some were of tin and square in shape; others were round, like canisters.

In one they found some tea and in another a small quantity of loaf sugar. There was no other food, except a few cracker crumbs in the bottom of a tin.

Leaving Inez to sit beside baby, Mildred next visited the room below.

Here the light was more dim, but she discovered a box of wax candles—two or three dozen in number—and a quantity of matches in a small iron safe. She tried these last and after several attempts managed to light one of them and with it light a candle. The matches were at least eight years old, but there was not a particle of dampness in the place and so they had not greatly deteriorated.

A broad slab of redwood, hinged and fastened to the wall by turn-buttons, was made to let down and serve as a table. When Mildred lowered it she found that it covered a small recess or cupboard in the wall, in which stood three tin cans. One was labeled "tomatoes" and the other two "corn."

Here was food, of a certain sort; but the cans were tightly soldered and there seemed to be no tool that might be used to open them. Although the place was littered with many small articles there was nothing else among them that especially interested the girl. Two sabers were crossed upon the wall over the table, and below them hung a big revolver. A panama hat, yellowed with age, hung upon a peg. A broom made of palm fiber stood in a corner.

Mildred returned to the upper floor, carrying with her several candles and some matches.

"Inez," said she, "we must make the best of our misfortune. I hope that before long we shall be rescued, both on baby's account and on our own. There are some tins of tomatoes and corn down stairs, but nothing that baby could eat. However, we shall suffer more from thirst than from hunger, as there is not a drop of water in the place."

Inez had been thinking during Mildred's absence.

"Can we not scream, and so make them hear us?" she asked.

"I have thought of that and we will make the attempt. The servants are all in the opposite wing, so it is useless to try to arouse their attention; but when Mr. and Mrs. Weldon return, with the others, they may be able to hear us and so rescue us."

"When will they be back?" Inez inquired.

Mildred considered this question.

"I heard them say they were to stay in town for luncheon, but Mrs. Weldon remarked that they would be back soon after. I think, Inez, they may already have returned and even now may be searching for us. Stay here, and I will go below, so as not to disturb baby, and call."

She went again down the steep stairs to the lower room where, standing near to the place where they had come through the wall, she uttered a sharp, shrill cry, such as she thought might penetrate the thick blocks of adobe. The sound echoed with startling reverberations through the secret chambers and baby Jane, wakening in affright, set up a series of such lusty screams that it seemed as if they ought to be heard a mile away.

Inez did her best to soothe and quiet the baby, but succeeded only when she had given little Jane the precious bottle of milk.

CHAPTER XV—MILDRED CONFIDES IN INEZ

Mildred had hastened upstairs in alarm at the pandemonium of sound her own cry had aroused, for the baby's screams also gave back a thousand echoes and these sent the little one into fresh paroxysms of terror.

"This won't do, at all," she said anxiously, when baby Jane had sobbed herself into a doze, with the bottle to comfort her. "If we scream again it will frighten the child to death."

"Perhaps they have heard us," suggested Inez, rocking Jane to and fro in her arms.

"Perhaps. Let us hope so," sighed Mildred.

Presently she went over to the couch and examined the condition of the bedding. The linen sheets had withstood the years very well, but the blankets and coverlets had a musty smell. She spread some of these out to air and then went back and sat beside Inez.

Together they watched the light fade until the narrow space was full of creeping shadows. The air began to grow chilly, so Mildred arranged the couch and they laid baby Jane upon it, covered her snugly with a blanket and drew the silk curtain to shield her eyes from the glare of the candles. They had lighted several of these, placing them in heavy brass candlesticks which they found ranged upon the shelves. Each of the girls took a blanket and folded it about her and then they sat down together to await their fate as patiently as they could.

They both realized, by this time, that their dilemma was likely to prove serious. Not a sound from within the house penetrated the adobe walls of their prison. They were unable to tell if their whereabout had yet been discovered.

"I think it best to wait until morning before we make any further effort to be heard," said Mildred. "Our cries would only distract baby and if our screams have not already attracted notice it would be folly to continue them. Anyway, let us try to be brave and patient. Something may happen to save us, before morning."

Even by the flickering candle-light the place was awesome and uncanny. Inez crept closer to Mildred's side, quite forgetting her former aversion for her companion. Because the sound of their own voices lent them a certain degree of courage they conversed together in low tones, talking on any subject that occurred to them.

At one time Inez broke an oppressive stillness by saying:

"Tell me about yourself—when you were a girl. And why did you leave here to go to New York?"

Mildred regarded the girl musingly. She felt a strong temptation to speak, to confide in some one.

"Will you keep my secret, Inez?" she asked.

"Yes; of course. I do not tell all I know," was the reply.

"If you told, it would drive me away from here," said Mildred.

Inez gave a start, remembering that a few hours ago she would have done anything to drive Mildred away. But, somehow, she had come to regard her companion in misfortune more favorably. A bond of sympathy had been established between them by this terrible experience they were now undergoing. Whatever their fate might be, Inez could not hate Mildred after this.

"I do not wish to drive you away," she asserted in a positive voice. "I will not tell your secret."

For a time Mildred mused silently, as if considering how to begin.

"My mother died when I was a baby," said she. "She was a Travers and lived on a ranch near here."

"I know the Travers Ranch," said Inez quickly. "But no Travers have live there in a long time."

"My mother lived there," continued Mildred, "until she married my father. Indeed, she lived there several years after, for I was born in the ranch house. But my mother's people—the Traverses—did not like my father, and when mother died he took me away to a house in Escondido. I think he was sent away, and the family sold the ranch and went back to England, where they had originally come from.

"In Escondido an old Mexican woman kept house for us. She was named Izbel."

"Ah!" cried Inez, nodding her head wisely; "I know." Then, as Mildred looked at her questioningly, she added: "Go on."

"My father was away from home much of the time. He traveled, and sometimes he took me with him into Mexico, and we went as far south as Matanzas, and once to Mexico City. That was when I was quite small, and I do not remember much about it. But often we came here to visit Señor Cristoval, with whom he had some secret business. I have seen him give my father big bags of golden coins, although everyone said he was a miser. I remember that at one time my father hid in this very wall for a day and a night, and officers came to the house and searched it, saying they were looking for a smuggler and had traced him here.

"But Señor Cristoval laughed at them and told them to examine the house thoroughly. This they did, and went away satisfied. Afterward my father came out of the wall and took me across the country to San Bernardino, where we stayed at a friend's house for several days. Finally Señor Cristoval came there to visit us and I heard him tell my father it would not be safe for him to return home and advised him to go far away. He also gave my father much money, and one curious thing which he said to him I never forgot. 'I will keep your fortune safely until you need it,' was his remark. 'I will hide it where no one will ever find it, any more than they could find you.'"

"Ah! then he hid your father's fortune in this place?" cried Inez eagerly.

Then her face fell. "But, no," she added. "We have look, and there is no fortune here."

Mildred sighed and continued her tale.

"After this Señor Cristoval shook my father's hand, and kissed me—for he was always fond of me—and went away. I never saw him again. My father and I traveled to New York and as I was then eleven years of age I became much troubled over our exile and begged to be told why it was not safe for us to stay in California. He explained to me that he had purchased laces and other goods in Mexico and brought them into the United States secretly, without paying the duty which the robbing government officials imposed. For that he said he was liable to be arrested and put in prison, and if I ever allowed the secret to escape me I would be the means of ruining him. I was a very sensitive child, and the importance of this great secret weighed upon me heavily. My father declared he had done no wrong, but I knew that the officers of the law were constantly searching for him and it so crushed me and destroyed my happiness that at twelve years of age I was as nervous, as suspicious and evasive as any old woman could be."

She paused and gave a little shudder. Said Inez, who had listened intently:

"I know now who you are. Your name is Mildred Leighton."

"You know that!" cried Mildred, amazed.

"Of course I know that, when I know your father was the great smuggler that the officers never could catch. I am told many stories about Leighton the smuggler, and old Izbel, who kept his house, is my aunt. Old Izbel say Señor Cristoval give Leighton the money to buy with, and Leighton give Señor Cristoval, who love money so much, half of all he make. But no one could ever prove that. Leighton was very clever man. No one could ever catch him."

Inez spoke admiringly, as if Mildred's father was a hero and Mildred had gained added prestige by being his daughter. But the other girl frowned and continued her story.

"In New York," she said, "we lived in a boarding house and I was sent to school. My father was not kind to me any more. He grew cross and gloomy and often would say if I told his secret he would kill me. I did not tell; I kept the secret safe locked in my heart and suffered agonies of apprehension for his sake, for I still loved him fondly. He now bought a little ship and began to make sea voyages to and from Cuba. He would not let me go with him and he only swore when I tried to get him to give up the wicked and dangerous life he was leading. Often he denounced Cristoval, who had in his possession valuable goods and money belonging to my father but would not give them up because he knew my father dared not go to California to get them.

"For years father continued to smuggle without being suspected. Then one morning I received a note asking me to come to the prison to see him. They had caught him at last and seized his ship, and he said there had been a fight in which several of the government agents had been shot, and one killed. My father did not shoot, he told me, but they would blame him for everything.

"He stayed in the prison for a month, and every day I went to see him. Then came the trial and he was sentenced to prison for life. They—they proved that he ordered his men to shoot," she added, lowering her head as if ashamed.

"Well, that was right," maintained Inez, cheerfully. "If they try to arrest him, Leighton was right to shoot."

"No, Inez, he was very wrong," replied Mildred sadly. "I would never be allowed to see my father after he was taken away, so they let us talk for the last time. He told me they had taken away all his money and he had nothing to give me, but that if I could manage to get to California old Señor Cristoval owed him much money and—and other things, and perhaps he would give it to me, although he had refused to give it to my father. Afterward they took him away to Sing Sing prison, and that was the last I ever saw of him, for a year later he died.

"I do not suppose, Inez, any girl was ever left with such a heritage of shame and trouble. You think me hard and cold; but can you blame me? Always I think some one will discover my secret, that they will say I am the daughter of Leighton the smuggler and point the finger of shame at me.

"I was a friendless girl with no money. The people at the boarding house would not let me remain and I took my little bundle and wandered out into the street in search of home and employment. It was then that a kind lady, a Mrs. Runyon, had pity on me and put me into a school for nurses. I was fifteen years old and big and strong for my age. At seventeen I was nursing in a charity hospital, but my father's disgrace had made me an outcast and prevented my obtaining situations with good families. Mrs. Runyon tried to help me but my story was too well known. I changed my name from Leighton to Travers, but even that did not bring me better luck.

"For two years longer I worked for a bare pittance, and then suddenly a ray of sunshine appeared. Miss De Graf came to the hospital where I was caring for an injured child and offered me a position with her cousin out here in California, where I had known the happiest days of my life. More than that, I found to my joy that I was coming directly to the old Cristoval house, for although Señor Cristoval was long since dead—as I had found out by writing him—I remembered the secret rooms and hoped I might find at least a part of my father's fortune still hidden there.

"Well," she added after a pause, "these are the rooms, and there is nothing of value left in them; this is the old Cristoval home, where my father was forced to hide from the law; this is the country where the officers hounded the hated smuggler like a dog and finally drove him away. And here is the girl, Inez, who has passed through all these scenes and to-day finds nothing in life worth living for."

Inez took her hand, shyly but tenderly.

"Meeldred," she said softly, "perhaps your life will end here. It will be strange, will it not, if that is so? But if we cannot get out, it makes a good story to die in this old den of the smuggler, your father. I will die with you;

but I do not mind—much. But Mees Jane—"

She broke off with a wail of anguish and Mildred said hastily:

"Inez, we must save the baby! And, if we do, we shall also save ourselves. Come; you, at least, have much to live for. You will care for the baby after I have gone far away, and you will be glad, then, that the hated Mildred is out of your life."

"But I do not hate you any more!" cried the Mexican girl protestingly. "I like you now, Meeldred. We will be friends, an' we will be happy together, if —if—"

"If what, Inez?"

"If we live to get out of this wall."

CHAPTER XVI—AN UNEXPECTED ARRIVAL

As the night advanced the two girls continued to talk, in low and subdued voices because of their anxiety and growing fears. They kept the candles trimmed, for the light lent them courage. They were not hungry, although they had eaten nothing since noon, but they were beginning to suffer from thirst.

The baby wakened with shrill screams and the only way to quiet her was to give her the bottle, which was now less than a third full. Mildred was in a quandary whether to withhold the remainder of the food from little Jane, so as to prolong her life as much as possible, or to allow the baby to eat what she desired, as long as any of the food remained. She finally decided on the latter course, hoping the morning would bring some one to their rescue.

After the little one was again hushed in slumber and cuddled in warm blankets on a seat beside them, the two imprisoned girls renewed their desultory conversation. They realized it must be long after midnight but Mildred avoided looking at her watch because that made the minutes drag so slowly.

Finally a dull sound from the other side of the wall reached their ears. It seemed that some one was pounding upon the adobe. Both girls sprang to their feet in excitement, their heads bent to listen. The pounding was not repeated but a voice was heard—a far-away voice—as of one calling.

Mildred answered the cry, at the top of her lungs, and immediately Inez followed with a shrill scream that roused a thousand echoes in the hidden passage. And now Toodlums joined the chorus, startled from her sleep and terrified by the riot of sound.

They tried to listen, but the baby's cries prevented anything else from being heard, so they devoted themselves to quieting little Jane. It took some time to do this, for the sobbing infant was thoroughly frightened, but finally

Inez succeeded in comforting her and the bottle of precious milk was sacrificed to put baby to sleep again.

By this time the sounds on the other side of the wall had ceased; but the girls were now full of eager hope, believing they had succeeded in letting their friends know they were imprisoned in the wall.

Within the hour more dull pounding began and this continued so regularly that Mildred told Inez the rescuers were surely trying to break through the adobe. They listened alertly to each blow and for a time forgot both thirst and fatigue in the excitement of the moment. Daybreak was near, for already a gray light was creeping in through the gratings overhead.

Suddenly a crash like a thunder-clap resounded from the end of the passage. From the gloomy recess behind the couch a man's form appeared, struck the bed, was rebounded by the springs into the air, turned a complete somersault and landed on the floor of the passage in a sitting position, facing the two startled nurses.

He did not seem to be hurt, but was evidently bewildered. He glared in amazement at the girls and they glared in amazement at him. Then, slowly, he turned his eyes to view his surroundings and blinked stupidly at the candles, the antique carved furniture, the baby bundled upon a cushioned seat and finally rested his eyes again upon the faces of the nurses.

"Why, it is Señor Bul-Run!" cried Inez, clapping her hands with joy. "He have come to save us."

"Pardon me," said the man, in a rather quavering falsetto, "I'm not sure whether I've come to save you or to share your peril. Where am I, please?"

"It is the hollow of the wall, sir," replied Mildred, who had never seen the big fellow before. "It is the secret apartment constructed by Señor Cristoval, who built this house."

"Well," said he, slowly getting upon his feet and with another curious glance around, "I can't say that I consider it a desirable place of residence.

Certainly it's no place for our precious Toodlums," and he bent over the sleeping babe and tenderly kissed its forehead. Then, straightening up, he said in as determined a tone as his high voice would permit: "We must find a way to get out of here!"

"Can't you get out the same way you got in?" asked Mildred.

He looked at her in perplexed astonishment.

"How did I get in?" he inquired.

"Don't you know?"

"I've no idea. I was sitting in the window of the blue room, resting, when there was a bang, whirligig, fireworks—and here I am, your uninvited guest."

"The blue room!" cried Mildred.

"Yes. Did you happen to notice my arrival? I don't mean its lack of dignity, but the direction I came from?"

"You came from somewhere behind that bed. I saw you strike the mattress and—and bound up again."

"To be sure. I remember bounding up again. I—I didn't care to stop, you see. I was anxious to—to—see if baby Jane was all right."

Mildred could not repress a smile, while Inez giggled openly.

"However," continued the big man, good-humoredly, "the direction affords us a clew. Pardon my absence for a moment while I investigate."

He took one of the candles, cautiously made his way over the couch and stood upon the oak chest at the end of the narrow chamber. Here he was able to examine the heavy planking set in the adobe, through which he had doubtless made his appearance but which now appeared as solid and immovable as the wall itself.

Runyon's first act was to pass the light of the candle carefully over every joint and edge, with the idea of discovering a spring or hinge. But no such thing seemed to exist. Then he took out his big jackknife and began prying.

When a blade snapped he opened another, only to break it in his vain twisting and jabbing. Finally he threw the now useless knife from him and began pounding with his fists upon the planking, at the same time shouting with the best voice he could muster. Perhaps the pounding might have been heard had not his friends at that moment been seeking for his mangled form in the garden, among the rose vines.

After listening in vain for a reply, Runyon came back to the girls, saying:

"This is certainly a singular occurrence. I came in as easily as I ever did anything in my life, I assure you; but the way out is not so easy. However, we won't have to endure this confinement long, for the boys are breaking down the wall in two places."

Then, in reply to their anxious questioning, he related the incidents of the night: how the discovery was made that Toodlums and her two nurses were missing; of the search throughout the country in automobiles; how the major had heard the "ghost" of baby Jane, which had given them their first intimation of the truth, and of the desperate and vain attempts made to get into the secret chamber.

Mildred, in return, explained the accident that had led to their imprisonment and of their failure to find any means of escape.

"There must be a way out, of course," she added, "for Señor Cristoval would never invent such clever and complicated ways of getting into this hollow wall without inventing other means of getting out."

"True enough," agreed Runyon; "but I can't see why he thought it necessary to make the means of getting *out* a secret. These rooms were probably built as hiding-places, and there are at least two separate entrances. But whoever hid here should be master of the situation and have no difficulty in escaping when the danger was over."

"Unless," said Mildred, thoughtfully, "the rooms were also intended as a prison."

"Well, perhaps that is it," said the man. "Old Cristoval may have thought the occasion would arise when he would like to keep one or more prisoners here, so he concealed the exits as carefully as the entrances. Let us admit, young ladies, that it's a first-class prison. But," his tone changing to one of kindly concern, "how have you stood this ordeal? You must be worn out with anxiety, and desperately hungry, too."

As he gazed into Mildred's face it occurred to him, for the first time, that Jane's new nurse was an interesting girl. She was not exactly beautiful, but— attractive. Indeed, at that moment Mildred was at her best, despite the night's vigil. The hard, defiant look had left her eyes for the first time in years, driven out by a train of exciting events that had led her to forget herself and her rebellion against fate, at least for the time being.

"We are not very hungry," she said, smiling at the big, boyish rancher, "but we are thirsty. I'd give anything for a good drink of water. And baby is now devouring the last few drops of her prepared food. When it is gone there is nothing here that she can eat."

"Well," said he, spurred to action by this report, "I'm going to explore this place carefully, for if we can manage to find a way out it will save Weldon and his men from ruining that wall, and also save time, for the blamed adobe is so hard and thick that it will still require hours for them to make a hole big enough to get us out."

CHAPTER XVII—THE PRODIGAL SON

With the added light that now came from the gratings in the ceiling every object in the upper room was plainly visible. Runyon began his inspection in a methodical manner, starting at one corner and eyeing the inner wall on every inch of its surface. He tested each block at its corners and edges. The girls watched him listlessly, for they expected no result, having covered the same methods themselves.

At length Runyon was obliged to abandon the wall in despair.

"The opening is there, of course," he said, "but that confounded Cristoval was too clever for us. If I had the rascal here now, I'd strangle him!"

As he stood in the center of the narrow space, looking around him, his eye fell upon the upholstered seats ranged along one side and he regarded them suspiciously. They were box-like affairs, with the surface of the covers padded and cushioned.

He reached down and lifted one of the lids. As he glanced within he uttered an exclamation of astonishment. The box was almost filled with bottles, lying regularly on their sides.

"Wine!" he cried. "Now, Miss—I don't remember to have heard your name—I shall be able to relieve your thirst."

"My name is Travers—Mildred Travers, sir; but I can't drink wine."

"Not to quench your thirst—just a few swallows?" he asked, taking a bottle and trying to remove the cork.

"Not a drop, even to save my life," she replied positively.

"But I will, Señor Runyon—I will!" cried Inez eagerly.

"Runyon!" exclaimed Mildred, stepping back in amazement and looking at the man rather wildly.

"Excuse me; haven't I introduced myself?" he asked, looking up. "Yes; my name's Runyon."

Something in her expression arrested his gaze and he regarded the girl curiously.

"Bulwer Runyon?" she said in a low voice.

He sat down on the box, holding the bottle between his knees.

"They christened me that. Very foolishly, I think. But what do you know of Bulwer Runyon?"

"Your mother—is—Martha Runyon?"

"To be sure—bless her heart! Ah, you know my mother, then, and that's how you have heard of me. But nothing good, from the dear old lady's lips, I'll be bound."

"She really loves you," replied Mildred quickly; "only—you have disappointed her."

"Indeed I have. I've always disappointed her, ever since I can remember."

"You were very extravagant," said Mildred in a reproachful tone.

"Yes; that was my fault. Father spoiled me; then he died and left all his fortune to mother. Quite right. But mother is pretty close with her money."

"Did she not pay all your debts?"

"Yes; but that was foolish. She reproached me for owing people, which was one of my pet recreations. So she paid the bills, bought me a ranch out here, shipped me into exile and washed her hands of me, declaring that the ranch was my sole inheritance and I must never expect another cent of her fortune. She proposes, I believe, to invest her surplus in charity. Nice idea, wasn't it?"

"It was very generous in her," declared Mildred.

"Was it? Well, that's a matter of opinion. But I regard her gift of this ranch as the first step to perpetual pauperdom. She tossed the land at me, shuffled me off, and then expected me to make a living."

"Can't you do that?" asked Mildred wonderingly.

"Make a living on a California ranch!" he said, as if astonished.

"Others do," she asserted.

"There is no other just like your humble servant," he assured her, again struggling with the cork. "I can't grow enough lemons—it's a lemon ranch she handed me—to pay expenses. The first year I decorated my estate with a mortgage; had to have an automobile, you know. The second year I put another plaster on to pay the interest of the first mortgage and a few scattering debts. Third year, the third patch; fourth year, the usual thing. Fifth year—that's this one—the money sharks balked. They said the ranch is loaded to its full capacity. So, I'll have to sell some lemons."

"Oh, I'm so sorry!" cried Mildred.

"So am I, thank you. Stupid thing, selling lemons. But the wolf's at the door and all I can do is shoot lemons at the brute. Lemons! Wasn't it tart of the dear mother to load me with such an acidulous estate? Perhaps she imagined it would make me assiduous—eh?"

"Your mother hoped you would turn over a new leaf and—and redeem your past," said the girl.

"Well, it's too late to do that now. I can't redeem the past without redeeming the ranch, and that's impossible," he declared with a grin. "But tell me, please, how you happen to be so deep in my mother's confidence."

Mildred hesitated, but reflected that she really owed him an explanation.

"She protected me when I was in trouble," she said softly.

"Ah; that's like the dear old girl. Do you know, I've an idea that when I'm down and out she'll relent and come to my assistance with a fatted calf? It would be just like her. I've known of others she befriended. Her hobby is to help poor girls. There was that Leighton girl, for instance, whose smuggling, murderous father was imprisoned for life. The poor little thing hadn't a friend in the world till mother took her in hand and put her in a training school for nurses. The mother wrote me how interested she was in that case. Her protege did her credit, it seems, for the child turned out a very good nurse, who—who —"

He suddenly paused, flushed red and stared at the girl uncertainly.

"You say your name is—Travers?" he asked.

"Yes," she replied, casting down her eyes.

"Not—Leighton?"

"Cannot you pull the cork, Señor Runyon? I am so thirsty!" cried Inez quickly, to save her friend from disclosing her secret. But big Runyon was bright enough, in spite of his peculiarities. He read Mildred's confusion and suspected the truth, but was too considerate to press the question.

"The cork is obstinate," said he; "so we won't argue with the thing," and he struck the neck of the bottle against a corner of the seat and broke it so neatly that not a drop of the contents was spilled. Then he took a cup from the shelf and poured out some of the wine.

"It's a native vintage," said he, "but it ought to be mellow and mild after all the years it has lain here."

Inez drank. The California Mexicans are accustomed to the native wines and consume them as freely as water. But Mildred, although again pressed to quench her thirst, steadfastly refused.

Runyon took a little of the wine, for he also was thirsty, and then he made an examination of the other seats. Some contained more wine; others were quite empty; but no water was discovered anywhere.

"Now I shall go below," said Runyon, "and see if I can unearth anything of importance there. Do you hear those dull sounds on the other side of the wall? They tell us that our friends are busy drilling the holes. It's wonderful how tough that adobe is."

Little Jane had awakened again and Inez took baby Jane in her arms and, with Mildred, followed Runyon down the stairs into the lower chamber. Here they watched his careful inspection of the room but did not hope for any favorable result.

"Here is food," he announced, as, having given up the idea of finding egress, he came upon the cans of tomatoes and corn.

"Yes; but we have no can-opener," replied Mildred; "and, unless the contents were cooked, they would not be eatable."

"I'm not thinking of the eatables," said Runyon, taking out a small pen-knife, for he had already ruined the larger one he always carried. "Tomatoes usually have a lot of liquid in the cans, a sort of watery juice which I am sure would help to relieve your thirst."

He began prying at the tin with a knife blade, but it was a heavy quality of plate, such as is rarely used nowadays, and resisted his attempt. Soon the blade of the frail tool snapped at the handle, and he tried the other blade. That, too, soon broke and Runyon regarded the can with a sort of wonder.

"It beats me," he said, shaking his head. "But I don't like to give up, and that tomato-juice would be of service if we could only get at it."

Looking around for another implement his eye spied the revolver hanging upon its peg.

"Ah! if that weapon is loaded I'll use a bullet as a can-opener," he exclaimed, and reaching up he removed the revolver from its place.

"Good; six cartridges, 32 caliber," said he. "Now, young ladies, if you can stand the noise, and the powder hasn't spoiled, I believe I can make a hole in that can which will allow the juice to run out."

"I don't care," said Inez, "but I will take Mees Jane upstairs, first."

"The sound will echo like a regular battle," said Mildred; "but as I am really thirsty and your suggestion of relief tempts me, I am willing to have you shoot the pistol."

Runyon placed the can upon the edge of the low hinged table, where it stood about waist high. When Inez had gone above with little Jane, the man took a position whereby he faced obliquely the outer wall and aiming at the tomatoes said:

"Better stop up your ears, Miss—Mildred."

She obeyed and he fired.

Even their anticipations could not prepare them for the wild riot of sound that followed the explosion. The bullet found its mark, for the can toppled and fell from the shelf and lay spilling its contents upon the floor. The bullet went farther and struck a crevice of the outer wall. A cloud of smoke for a moment obscured their view and Mildred, regarding the tomato-can, cried out:

"Oh, pick it up! Pick it up, quick! It is spilling."

Runyon made no reply. He was staring straight ahead, in a dazed, bewildered way, and now Mildred's eyes followed his.

The smoke was rolling out of a large aperture in the outer wall. Three huge blocks of adobe, neatly joined together, had swung outward, moved by a secret spring which the bullet had released.

Through the grim prison wall they were looking out at the sunshine that flooded the rose garden.

Mildred sank to her knees, sobbing with joy. Big Runyon walked to the staircase.

"Hi, there, Inez!" he called. "Come down here and take Toodlums to her mother. I'll bet a button she'll be jolly glad to see that kid again!"

CHAPTER XVIII—LACES AND GOLD

At four o'clock in the afternoon Patsy rubbed her eyes, yawned and raised her head from her pillow.

"Dear me!" she sighed, "I'm tired yet, but this sleeping in the daytime is unnatural. I wonder if Beth is awake."

She went to the door of the adjoining room, opened it and found her cousin dressing.

"Do you suppose anyone else is up?" she inquired.

"See there," replied Beth, pointing through the window.

Patsy saw. Mr. Runyon was seated on a garden bench in earnest conversation with Mildred Travers.

"Didn't he go home this morning, after the excitement was over?" she asked.

"No," replied Beth. "Mr. and Mrs. Hahn drove their car home, but our interesting neighbor at the north, Mr. Bul Run, declared there was nothing at his own ranch half so enticing as a bed here. He's a bachelor, it seems, and leads rather a lonely life. So Arthur gave him a room and he went to bed; but it seems he has had his sleep out and is indulging in other recreations."

Patsy was eyeing the couple in the garden.

"Mr. Runyon seems to have struck up a friendship with your protégé Mildred," she observed.

"Yes," answered Beth. "You know he was shut up in the wall with her and Inez for awhile and the adventure must have made them feel well acquainted. Wasn't that imprisonment a most peculiar thing, Patsy?"

"Very peculiar. I haven't had much time to think about it, for as soon as

Toodlums was safe in Louise's arms I went to bed. But it occurs to me to wonder how Mildred Travers knew so much of the secrets of this absurd old house and why she ventured to explore the hidden rooms in our absence. Put that with the fact that she lived in these parts as a girl, and with her eagerness to come out here—don't you remember her fervent 'thank heaven'?—and it seems the whole mystery isn't unraveled yet; it's only getting more tangled."

Beth was thoughtful for a time.

"I am sure Mildred will have some explanation to make," she said presently. "Don't let us judge her just yet, Patsy. And I advise you to get dressed, for there's Louise wheeling the baby, and perhaps everyone else is downstairs but us."

"Louise and baby both slept all through that awful night," remarked Patsy, again yawning. "No wonder they're up and around and looking bright and happy." But she took her cousin's hint and dressed so rapidly that she descended the stairs only a few moments after Beth did.

Uncle John, the major and Arthur were in the court, smoking and sipping coffee. The events of the past night were still being earnestly discussed by them and much speculation was indulged in concerning the rooms in the hollow wall and the uses to which they had been put during the pioneer days when Cristoval constructed them, and even afterward when his son, the last owner, had occupied the premises.

"The entire ranch," said Arthur, "as well as this house, was sold by the executors appointed by the court, for it seems that Cristoval had no heirs in this country. The money was sent over to Spain and divided among a host of relations, the executors were discharged, and that ended the matter as far as the law is concerned. But I am sure the secret of the wall was at that time unknown to any, for otherwise the furniture in those narrow rooms, some of which is expensive and valuable on account of its unique carving, and the bins of wine and other truck, would have been sold with the other 'personal possessions.' I bought this place of a man who had purchased it at the executors' sale but never has lived in it. All the rooms were stripped bare, which goes to prove that the hidden recesses in the walls were unknown. Now, the question is, do I legally own the contents of that wall, or don't I?"

"I stepped into the rooms, this morning, with the others, but merely glanced around a bit," said Mr. Merrick. "I've an idea you may rightfully claim whatever is there. The value of such old, odd pieces is arbitrary and they wouldn't total enough at an auction sale to bother about. My idea, Arthur, is that you remove whatever you care to retain, stop up the rat holes, and then seal up the place forever."

"I suppose," remarked the major, "those hollow places in the wall were of real value in the days of wild Indians and murdering highwaymen. But, as John Merrick says, they're of no use to anyone now, but rather a source of danger."

"Was that door left open?" asked Patsy.

"Yes; and I put a brace against it, so it couldn't close and shut us out," replied Arthur.

"That doesn't matter; Mildred knows the way in," said Beth. "The whole trouble was that Inez closed the door behind them and they couldn't manage to get out again."

Mr. Merrick sipped his coffee reflectively.

"That girl," said he, "ought to explain how she knows so much—and so little."

"And what she was doing in the secret rooms," added the major.

"She'll do that," piped a high voice, and in sauntered Mr. Runyon and sat down to pour himself some coffee. "I've just left Miss—er—er—Travers, and she has decided to tell you all her whole story, frankly and without reservation, and then she wants to ask your advice."

"Whose advice?" demanded Arthur.

"Everybody's advice. She asked mine, a little while ago, and I told her to put it up to the crowd. The poor thing has had a sad history and there's a bit of romance and tragedy connected with it; but she has been quite blameless. I haven't known you people long, but I'll bank on your generosity and fairness, and that's what I told the poor girl."

"Where is she now?" asked Patsy.

"In the garden with Mrs. Weldon and Toodlums. They'll all be here presently."

The little group remained silent and thoughtful until Louise entered wheeling the baby in her cab and followed by Mildred Travers. The nurse's face was white and troubled but she had acquired a new attractiveness for the reason that her eyes had softened and were now pleading instead of defiant.

Inez came running from the nursery to take baby, but Louise would not let little Jane go. Although she had escaped much of the past night's misery, thanks to Dr. Knox's quieting powders, the young mother was still unnerved and liked to have the child where she could see it. So Inez sat on a bench and held Jane, who was the least concerned of anyone over her recent peril and fortunate escape.

The court was shady, cool and quiet. Those assembled eyed Mildred curiously and expectantly, so that she was really embarrassed at first. Beth, who felt in a measure responsible for this waif of a great city, because she had been instrumental in bringing her here, gently led Mildred to a beginning of her story by asking a few questions that afforded the girl an opening.

The entire party listened gravely to the recital, for only Inez, among those present, had ever heard any part of the strange tale before.

Mildred told practically the same story she had related to the Mexican girl the night before, but went more into details and explained more fully her girlhood acquaintance with Señor Cristoval.

"He was an unusual man," said she; "aged and white-haired, as I remember him, and always dressed in white flannels, which threw his dark skin into sharp relief. He lived alone in the house, having but one man-servant to do all the work, cook his meals and cater to his slightest whim."

"Miguel Zaloa," said Inez in a low voice.

"Cristoval was not popular," said Mildred, "for he loved money so well that he was reputed to be a miser. It was this love of money, I think, that induced him to go into partnership with my father in his illegal smuggling enterprises. Cristoval furnished the money and when my father had slipped across the border with his bales of rare laces, they were hidden in the hollow wall until they could be forwarded to San Francisco and sold.

"And this brings me to a relation of my present interest in this house," she continued. "When we escaped from California a large lot of very valuable Mexican laces which belonged exclusively to my father was hidden in the wall. The sale of a former lot of smuggled goods had resulted in a large profit and Cristoval had received a bank draft for the amount, one half of which was due my father. When we last saw Cristoval at San Bernardino, before we left for New York, he promised my father to cash the draft and send him the proceeds. This he never did, although he advanced my father, at that time, a sum of money from other sources to pay our expenses until we could establish ourselves in the east.

"To avoid suspicion, my father always allowed Cristoval to bank the partnership money, drawing on the rich Spaniard from time to time for what he required. Father told me that altogether Cristoval owed him nine thousand dollars, besides the bale of laces, valued at ten thousand more. He wrote many times to demand this money, using a cipher they had arranged between them, but his letters were never answered. I know now that Cristoval died soon after we went to New York, so whoever got the letters, being unable to read the secret cipher, of course ignored them.

"Just as Leighton was being taken to prison, the last time I ever saw him, he told me to find some way to come here and get the money. He said that if

Cristoval was dead, as he then suspected, the secret of the wall was still safe, for the old man had vowed never to disclose it. He thought I would find the laces still hidden in the wall, and perhaps the money."

"Did you look to see, while you were there?" asked Arthur Weldon.

"Yes. There is no evidence of any property that I could rightfully claim."

It was a strange recital, and a fascinating one to those who heard it.

"Who would think," said Patsy, "that in this prosaic age we would get so close to a real story of smuggling, hidden treasure and secret recesses in walls? It smacks more of the romantic days of past centuries."

"We must not forget," replied Louise, "that of all our numerous states California has the most romantic history. It wasn't so long ago that the Spanish don flourished in this section and even yet it is more Spanish than American except in the big cities."

"As for smuggling," added Runyon, "that is going on to-day—as merrily as in the days of the famous Leighton, if on a smaller scale. I've some choice cigars over at my ranch that have never paid duty, and I've an order with the smuggler for more. So, after all, there's nothing very astonishing in Mildred Leighton's story."

"The wall we have practical evidence of," said Uncle John. "I suppose it will hold its secret rooms for many years to come, for these adobe dwellings are practically fire-proof and are built to defy time."

"But about Mildred's fortune," cried Patsy. "Don't you suppose it is hidden, after all, some place in the wall?"

"From what I have heard of Cristoval," said Arthur in a reflective tone, "he was not considered a dishonest man, but rather miserly and grasping."

"My father," explained Mildred, "trusted him fully until we went away and could get no answer to his letters. The old Spaniard was very fond of me, also, and he would hold me in his arms and say that one day I would be a rich lady, for my father and he were both making my fortune. I was very young, as you know, but I never forgot that statement."

"Suppose," suggested the major, "we make another and more thorough search of those secret rooms."

"We will do that," replied Arthur promptly. "It is too late to undertake the task to-night, but we will begin it right after breakfast to-morrow morning. Inez, I wish you would slip down to the quarters and ask Miguel to come and help us. Tell him to be here at nine o'clock."

The girl nodded, gave the baby to Mildred and stole quietly out of the court.

CHAPTER XIX—INEZ AND MIGUEL

Inez found Miguel Zaloa smoking his cigarette among the orange trees. He was quite alone and looked at the girl in an expectant way as she approached.

"Oh, Miguel!" she cried. "I tell you a secret. Of course it is no secret any more, for now they all know it, up there at the house. Meeldred Travers, the girl from New York, is not Meeldred Travers. She is the child of Leighton the smuggler—she is Meeldred Leighton!"

The old ranchero stood as if turned to stone, but he bit his cigarette in two and it fell unnoticed upon the ground. While Inez regarded him with disappointment, because he had exhibited no emotion at hearing the wonderful news, Miguel turned his back and mechanically walked away through a row of trees. A dozen paces distant he halted and again stood motionless for the space of a full minute. Then he swung around and with slow, hesitating steps returned to Inez.

"You say—she—ees Meeldred Leighton?" he asked, as if he thought he had not heard aright.

"Of course. Don't you remember, Miguel? She say, when she used to come here, a little girl, with Leighton the great smuggler, you did know her. It was then you served Señor Cristoval, at the big house."

He nodded, his dark eyes fixed upon her face but displaying no expression.

"Leighton is dead," continued Inez, delighted to be able to gossip of all she had heard. "They put him in a prison an' he died. So Meeldred was ashamed of her father's bad name an' call herself Travers. She is poor, an' that is why she come here as nurse, so she can find the money that belong to her."

Miguel suddenly seized her wrist in a powerful grip.

131

"What money?" he demanded.

"Don't; you hurt my arm! It is the money Señor Cristoval owed her father. Take your hand away, Miguel Zaloa!"

Slowly he released her.

"Where will she find thees money?" he asked.

"She does not know. Perhaps it is not here at all. But there was a great heap of laces, worth much money, which Señor Cristoval hid in the wall to keep for Leighton."

Miguel laughed. He seemed suddenly to have regained his equanimity. He began rolling another cigarette.

"They will be old, by now, thees lace," said he.

"A lace is better when it is old," asserted the girl.

The man paused, looked at the half-made cigarette and tossed it away. Then he glanced around to see if they were observed and taking Inez' arm— gently, this time—he led her away from the path and into a thicket of orange trees.

"Thees Meeldred," he said in soft tones, "you hate."

"No, no! I do not hate her now. I love Meeldred."

"So!" he said, drawing in his breath and regarding the girl with surprise. "You tell me once she is witch-woman."

"I am wrong," declared Inez earnestly. "She is good. She have been poor an' friendless, all because of her father, the noble smuggler Leighton. But see, Miguel; I have been all night shut up in the wall with her. We talk, an' I learn to know her better. I do not hate Meeldred any more—I love her!"

"Sit down," said the old man, pointing to a hillock beside a tree. Inez obeyed, and he squatted on the ground facing her and coolly rolled another cigarette. "Tell me more about thees girl—Leighton's girl," he said.

Inez related Mildred's story as well as she was able, exaggerating such romantic details as appealed to her fancy, but showing unbounded sympathy for her new friend. The aged ranchero listened intently, nodding his white head now and then to show his interest. When the girl had finished he smoked for a time in silence.

"What Meeldred do now?" he inquired.

"They will hunt in the wall, to-morrow, to find the lace," she replied. "Meest Weldon say for you to come to the house at nine o'clock, in morning, to help them."

"Meest Weld say that?"

"Yes. But we have search already—Meeldred an' me—an' Meest Bul-Run have search, an' no lace is there. I am sure of that. I am sure no money is there, too. So Meeldred mus' stay as nurse all her life an' help me take care of Mees Jane."

Miguel pondered this.

"B'm'by Mees Jane grow up," said he. "What can Leighton's daughter do then?"

"How can I tell that?" answered Inez, shaking her head. "Always poor people mus' work, Miguel. Is it not so?"

"Rich people mus' work, too," continued the Mexican girl dreamily, as she embraced her drawn-up legs and rested her chin upon her knees. "Was old Señor Cristoval more happy than we, with all the money he loved? No! Meest Weldon works; Meest Hahn works; even Meest Bul-Run works—sometime. If one does not work, one is not happy, Miguel; an' if one mus' work, money makes not any difference. So, when Meeldred find she is still poor, an' has no money an' no laces, like she hope for, she will work jus' the same as ever, an' be happy."

"I, too, work," remarked the old man. "I have always work."

"If you had much money, Miguel, you would still work."

"Yes."

"You would not care for money; not you. It would not do you any good. It would not change your life."

"No."

Again they sat in silence, as if reflecting on this primitive philosophy. Finally Inez said:

"You remember Leighton, Miguel?"

"Yes. He was good man. He make much money for Señor Cristoval an' for heemself. Sometime I see them count gold—ten pieces to Señor Cristoval, ten pieces to Leighton—to divide even. Then Leighton will throw me a gold-piece an' say: 'That for you, Miguel, because you are faithful an' true.'"

"An' Señor Cristoval, did he throw the gold-piece to you, also?"

"No."

"What did you do with the gold Leighton give you, Miguel?"

The old man shrugged his shoulders. "Tobacco. Some wine. A game of card."

"An' were you faithful an' true, as Leighton say?"

He looked at her long and steadily.

"What you theenk about that, Inez?"

"When people talk about Miguel Zaloa, they always say he is good man. I hear Meest Weldon say: 'Miguel is honest. I would trust Miguel with all I have.'"

"Meest Weld say that?"

"Yes."

"Well?"

"I think you are sometime honest, sometime not; like I am myself,"

134

replied the girl.

The old man rose and led the way back to the path.

"To be always honest is to be sometime foolish," he muttered on the way. "Tell Meest Weld I will be there, like he say, at nine o'clock."

CHAPTER XX—MR. RUNYON'S DISCOVERY

Sing Fing excelled himself at the dinner that evening, which was a merry meal because all dangers and worries seemed to belong to the past. Also it was, as Uncle John feelingly remarked, "the first square meal they had enjoyed since the one at Castro's restaurant." Of course Runyon stayed, because he was to help search the wall the next day, and as the telephone had been repaired Louise called up Rudolph and Helen Hahn and begged them to drive over and help them celebrate at the festive board.

So the Hahns came—although they returned home again in the late evening—and it was really a joyous and happy occasion. Inez brought in the baby, which crowed jubilantly and submitted to so many kisses that Patsy declared she was afraid they would wear the skin off Toodlum's chubby cheeks unless they desisted.

Mildred had gone to her room immediately after her confession in the court and Louise had respected her desire for privacy and had ordered her dinner sent in to her.

As they all sat in the library, after dining, in a cosy circle around the grate fire, they conversed seriously on Mildred Leighton and canvassed her past history and future prospects.

"I cannot see," said Beth, always the nurse's champion, "that we are called upon to condemn poor Mildred because her father was a criminal."

"Of course not," agreed Patsy, "the poor child wasn't to blame."

"These criminal tendencies," remarked the major gravely, "are sometimes hereditary."

"Oh, but that's nonsense!" declared Uncle John. "We can't imagine Mildred's becoming a smuggler—or smuggleress, or whatever you call it. That hard, cold look in her eyes, which we all so thoughtlessly condemned, was merely an indication of suffering, of hurt pride and shame for the disgrace that had been thrust upon her. I liked the girl better to-day, as with blazing cheeks she told of all her grief and struggles, than ever before since I knew her."

"The expression of the eye," said Arthur, "is usually considered an infallible indication of character."

"That's a foolish prejudice," asserted Patsy, whose own frank and brilliant eyes were her chief attraction.

"I do not think so, dear," objected Louise. "The eyes may not truly indicate character, but they surely indicate one's state of mind. We did not read the hard look in Mildred's eyes correctly, I admit, but it showed her to be on guard against the world's criticism, resentful of her hard fate and hopeless in her longing for a respectable social position. She realized that were her story known she would meet with sneers and jeers on every side, and therefore she proudly held herself aloof."

"But now," said Patsy, "circumstances have changed Mildred's viewpoint. She found that our knowledge of her story only brought her sympathy and consideration, and when she left us I noticed that her eyes were soft and grateful and full of tears."

Big Runyon had listened to this conversation rather uneasily and with evident disapproval. Now he said, in as positive a tone as his unfortunate voice would permit:

"That girl's a corker, and I'm proud of her. In the first place, my mother is a shrewd judge of character. You can't fool her about a person's worth; just see how accurately she judged *my* character! When the dear old lady—whose only fault is being so close-fisted—picked up Mildred Leighton and defended her, that act vouched for the girl's worth beyond dispute. Mrs. Runyon—bless her stingy old heart!—never makes a mistake. Just think of it: she actually spent money in giving Mildred an education as a trained nurse. To my mind that settled the girl's character for all time. Now, I don't care a continental whether she finds any smuggled laces or not; she needs a friend, and now that she is away from my mother's care *I'm* going to be that friend."

"Oh, Bul!" cried Louise with lively interest, "are you in love?"

"Me? At my age? Cer-tain-ly not!"

"How old are you?"

"Thirty."

"Old enough to know better," said Uncle John.

"Old enough to need a wife to care for him," suggested Helen Hahn.

"Honest Injun, Run; aren't you a little soft on Mildred?" asked Rudolph.

"Well, perhaps a little; but it's nothing like that currant-jelly, chocolate bonbon, glucose-like feeling which I've observed is the outward demonstration of love."

"Oh, well; marry the girl and be done with it, then," laughed Arthur.

"And rob me of my nurse?" protested Louise.

"Runyon needs a nurse as much as Jane. In fact, he's a much bigger baby."

Mr. Runyon accepted all this jollying with calm indifference.

"The days of chivalry are over," he sighed. "If a fellow tries to protect a maiden in distress, they think he wants to marry her."

"Don't you?" asked Patsy, in a sympathetic tone.

"Why, I hadn't thought of it before; but it wouldn't be a half-bad idea," he confessed. "Ranch life is a bit lonely without women around to bother one."

"You are all talking foolishly," observed Beth, who was not romantic. "Mildred might object to washing Mr. Runyon's dishes."

"Why, yes; I believe she would," said Mr. Runyon. "I'm sure she disapproves of my character; that's why I respect her judgment, so highly. She didn't seem at all interested in those various mortgages, when I mentioned them; and what else have I to offer a wife?"

Even the cosy library could not hold them very late, for none had been fully restored by the sleep obtained during the day. Bed seemed more alluring than a grate fire and when the Hahns went home the party broke up, to meet again at an eight o'clock breakfast.

As soon as the meal was over Arthur Weldon announced that the first business of the day would be an examination of the secret rooms in the wall of the old East Wing.

"And this must be a thorough and final inspection of the place," he added. "We must satisfy ourselves and Mildred Travers, without the shadow of a doubt, that we have inventoried every blessed thing in those rooms— even to the rats and beetles."

"That's right," approved Mr. Merrick. "Let us do the job once and for all. We've plenty of time at our disposal and there are enough of us with sharp eyes to ferret out every mystery of the place. In Mildred's interest we must be thorough."

In the court they found old Miguel, sitting motionless and patient. He was carefully dressed in his best clothes and wore a red necktie, "just as if," said Patsy, "he was going to a party instead of delving in dusty places."

The ranchero arose and made his master and mistress one of his best bows. Then he waited silently for instructions.

Beth went to Mildred's room and brought the girl to join the searchers, for this undertaking had been planned on her account. Her face wore an anxious look, for although she was not very hopeful of results it was the last chance of her securing any of her father's personal possessions. Otherwise she greeted the party with modesty and with gentle dignity and had never seemed to them more womanly or agreeable.

Together they left the court and proceeded to the nursery. There were no laggards and everyone except the servants was determined to have a part in the fascinating investigation.

Mildred explained to them the manner in which she had first entered the wall, putting in action the secret method taught her as a girl by Cristoval and demonstrating the mechanism before their very eyes. They entered the lower chamber, one by one, and this time the adobe door was not closed behind them, although the light of broad day now flooded the place through the opening discovered by Runyon. This opening led into the garden and was half choked with rose vines. The series of swinging blocks had been propped back against the outer wall to insure a ready exit in case of accident.

And now they eagerly set to work to pry into every crack and corner of the place. The main idea was to find some secret cavity or cupboard in the wall which might contain the missing laces or other valuables. With this in view they had brought levers and pries and all sorts of tools that might be of service.

The girls were mainly useful in taking up and turning the matting, now somewhat decayed by age, and investigating those nooks and shelves already discovered. But they found little more than Mildred had done during her first exploration, and the men who were testing the wall met with no encouragement at all. Aside from the two cleverly constructed openings—one into the nursery and one into the garden—the blocks which composed the wall seemed every one solid and immovable and resisted every attempt to wrest them from their places.

After more than two hours of industry, during which every man believed he had examined every block, they were forced to abandon the lower chamber and ascend the steep stairs to the upper one.

"This," said Arthur, looking around him, "seems far more promising. Let us give the floor our first attention, for it is not over the lower room but to one side of it. It strikes me that the builder would be quite likely to make a secret pocket in the floor."

Following this advice they attacked the blocks of the floor with pry and crowbar, but found nothing to reward them. Old Miguel worked steadily and did whatever he was told, but displayed no particle of enthusiasm, or even of interest.

After the floor, the walls were examined, one by one, from floor to ceiling. The panel on the inner wall, which had baffled both Mildred and Runyon on that eventful night of their imprisonment, suddenly disclosed its secret when accidentally pressed on opposite corners at the same time. It slipped down and discovered a similar panel beyond it, which was operated by a spring placed in plain sight. Releasing this, they found they were looking into the vacant second story room which they had once before unsuccessfully searched.

So this was one way from the house into the upper chamber of the wall. Of course there was another way—that through which Runyon had been so abruptly precipitated. In order to find this the more readily, they sent the big rancher into the blue room and asked him to take the same position in the window he had on the night of his disappearance. This he did, pushing against the planking that boxed the window, with both elbows and with his back and shoulders, but without result. Finally, in his attempts, he inadvertently struck the opposite panel with his heel, and the response was startling. The panel, at his back, being released, fell backward without warning and for the second time Runyon tumbled unawares into the chamber of the wall. As soon as his body had fallen through, the panel slammed into place again, urged by a very powerful steel spring, but the major, who had been in the blue room to watch Runyon, had caught the trick and the mystery was solved.

As for Mr. Runyon, he again fell upon the bed and rebounded, knocking over both Mr. Merrick and Miguel as he alighted in the narrow chamber, but fortunately not injuring either of them.

A little dazed by his second precipitation, the big rancher stared a moment and then slapped his thigh a mighty stroke.

"I have it—I have it!" he cried.

"It occurs to me," said Uncle John, a little resentfully, "that you deserve all you've got, and more. It's a wonder you didn't break your neck."

"What have you, Run?" asked Arthur.

"I've found the laces." "What?—

where?" they exclaimed.

"In the blue room, or on the way down?" added Beth sarcastically.

"After I got down," he answered. "What fools we have all been!"

"Will you kindly explain, Mr. Runyon?" asked Mildred, very earnestly.

"I will. It's simple enough. Just look at that bed."

"The bed!" And now every eye was turned upon the couch.

"Of course," said Runyon. "There's something more than a mere mattress and springs. I've tumbled onto the thing twice, and I ought to know."

CHAPTER XXI—A FORTUNE IN TATTERS

Already Arthur was pulling off the bedding and piling it upon the floor. They stood back of him in an excited group, every head craned forward to watch his movements.

Off came the pillows—blankets—sheets—finally the mattress. This last, a thin cotton affair, left a trail of fuzzy, lint-like debris behind it and disclosed on removal a canvas cover that had been spread underneath. The canvas, which was about on a level with the boxed-in bed frame, was as full of holes as a Swiss cheese and especially toward the center the weave had become disintegrated and given away to a dusty pulp.

"Rats!" exclaimed Uncle John, whose head was thrust between the shoulders of the major and Runyon.

As if his cry had been a summons, out sprang a huge gray rodent and the girls pushed back with loud screams as the dreaded beast struck the floor and scurried away down the passage. Another and another followed it, and now Louise, Patsy, Beth, Mildred and Inez were all dancing on top the seats, wrapping their skirts about their ankles and whooping like a tribe of Indians.

Amid this wild hullabaloo, which struck terror to the hearts of the brave men assembled, because at the instant they were too bewildered to realize what caused it, some six or eight monstrous rats leaped from the tattered canvas which covered the bed and vanished down the stairs.

Arthur put his hand down to raise the canvas and jumped back as he unearthed a nest of smaller vermin, squirming here and there in blind endeavors to escape their disturbers. Runyon brought a deep brass bowl from a shelf and dumped the small rats into it, standing by to capture others as they appeared.

Gradually Weldon drew back the cover and as he did so the truth of

Runyon's prophecy was apparent. The entire space boxed in by the carved bed-frame, from the floor to its upper edge, was packed solidly with valuable laces. That is, it had once been solidly packed, but now the rats had eaten tunnels and nests and boulevards through the costly laces in every direction. It was a scene of absolute ruin. However precious this collection might once have been, in its present state it was not worth a copper cent.

The party gazed upon the sight with mingled awe and astonishment. Regret for the destruction of the beautiful fabrics at first rendered them oblivious to the fact that the inheritance of Mildred Leighton was at last recovered—only to be proved worthless.

Arthur dragged out a few scraps and spread them upon the floor, thereby exhibiting portions of the beautiful patterns of the various pieces. Then, hoping to find some that had escaped the ruthless teeth of the rats, he and Runyon began pulling at the heap and working downward toward the floor. Just a few small pieces were found intact, but these were of slight value. Practically the entire lot was irretrievably ruined.

Scarcely a word was spoken as the investigation proceeded. Beth had clasped one of Mildred's hands and Patsy the other, but neither dared look in the poor girl's face, for they dreaded the poignant disappointment sure to reign there.

But after the first shock, Mildred bore up bravely. She had not expected, in the beginning, any tangible result; still it was very bitter to find her long sought fortune and realize that it amounted to nothing.

They sat around upon the benches, or leaning against the wall, and stared at the ruined laces with various emotions, the keenest being regret for the loss of so much beautiful handwork and sympathy for Mildred Leighton.

Suddenly Runyon broke the silence.

"This discovery is too thundering bad for mere words," he said with feeling; "but Miss Travers—Mildred—must know we're all as sorry as she is. She was right about the laces, but the laces are all wrong. This sad exhibit reminds me of my own perverse mortgages, and my mortgages remind me of something else. Mildred," he added, turning to the girl in a dogged and rather shamefaced way, "I'm going to hold a private conversation with you right here before our good friends, for I know every one of them will back me up. Eh?" he questioned, glancing around the group.

There were some smiles, but many nods. As if encouraged, Runyon proceeded:

"This settles the question of your fortune. It's gone—vanished into scraps. You're a poor girl, now, with no glittering prospects, so what I'm going to say won't seem quite so selfish as it would otherwise. In fact, had these laces been perfect, they would have rendered me dumb. As it is, here stand two impecunious ones—you and I. Between us we haven't much more than enough to fry a fish, in solid cash, but among my encumbrances are a delightful little bungalow, nicely furnished, and a lot of lemon trees that can be coaxed to buy us groceries and ordinary comforts. I'm a lonely fellow, Mildred, and I need a companion. Will you marry me, and look after that bungalow?"

This extraordinary proposal was heard in breathless silence. The men were astounded, the girls delighted. Every eye turned curiously upon Mildred Travers, who regarded the big rancher with frank wonder, a wan smile upon her pallid features.

"You do not say you love me," she suggested, striving through mild banter to cover her confusion.

"Well, isn't that implied?" he answered. "No one would propose to a girl he didn't love, would he?"

"You have only known me two days."

"Two days and seven hours. But mother endorsed you and I'll bank on her judgment."

"When the mortgages come due, there won't be any bungalow," she continued.

"Don't you believe it," cried Runyon, earnestly. "With you to work for, I'll make those tart old lemons pay the interest and a good income besides. In fact, if we live long enough, we may even manage to reduce the mortgages. You see, I've been extravagant and foolish, but it was because I had no aim in life. The minute you say 'yes,' I'm a reformed character."

She shook her head and the smile faded from her face.

"Don't think me ungrateful, Mr. Runyon," she said quietly. "Unusual and —and—peculiar—as this proposal is, I believe you are sincere in what you say. But you are influenced just now by pity for me and I assure you I am quite capable of earning my own living."

"But—oh, Mildred—-he's so lonely," cried Patsy, impulsively.

"I'm sorry for that," she said, "but it is not my fault."

"It will be, though, if you refuse," declared Runyon.

"I fear I must."

"I see," he said with a sigh. "Mother endorsed you, but she didn't endorse me. You've heard some tough yarns about me—all true as gospel— and you're prejudiced. I don't know as I blame you. If I were a girl I'd hesitate to reform such a desperate character, I'm sure. But I've the notion there's the making of a decent fellow in me, if the right workman undertakes the job."

She looked at him earnestly, now—very earnestly. In spite of the squeaky voice and the inopportune time he had chosen for such a serious proposal, there was an innate manliness and ingenuousness in his attitude, as he stood there unabashed and towering above the other men, that seemed to her admirable and impressive. Both Beth and Patsy were reflecting that a girl might do much worse than to accept Bulwer Runyon as a mate.

Said Mildred, still speaking in the same quiet and composed voice:

146

"I will give you a positive answer in three days, Mr. Runyon. That delay is mere justice to us both."

"Thank you," he said. "Shall we fuss with these tattered laces any longer? It hardly seems worth while."

Now that the strain of the situation was removed they all began chattering volubly in order to give countenance to Mildred. Runyon seemed not to need such consideration.

Old Miguel had witnessed and overheard this scene from the background and his bright black eyes had roamed restlessly from the girl's face to Runyon's as if trying to read their true feelings. The discovery of the laces had not drawn any exclamation from the ancient ranchero, whose stolid expression nothing seemed able to disturb. As the others filed down the stairs and out of the recess in the wall, into the roomy nursery, old Miguel followed imperturbable and serene as ever. In the court he touched his hat to his master.

"I go now, Meest Weld?" he asked.

"Yes. Thank you, Miguel, for your help."

"I thank you, too," said Mildred, stepping forward to take the Mexican's hand. "I remember you well, Miguel. In the old days you often took care of me while my father and Señor Cristoval talked. Don't you remember?"

He nodded, his eyes fixed full upon her face.

"Once a friend, always a friend, Miguel," she continued brightly. "Even to-day you have been trying to help me, and I am grateful. Some time we will have a good talk together about the old days."

Then he went away, and if one who knew old Miguel Zaloa could have followed him, his actions would have caused surprise.

First he wandered deep into the orange groves, where—when absolutely alone—he began muttering excitedly. At times he would kick his booted foot viciously against a tree-trunk, regardless of the impact that numbed his toes and sent a tingle up his legs. After a time this remarkable exhibit of passion subsided and for the period of half an hour he stood quite motionless, staring straight before him and seeing nothing. Then he started off through the groves, climbed the fence into the lane and marched away through miles and miles of the surrounding country.

It was growing dark when Miguel at last appeared at the quarters, growling at the men and ordering them to get into the groves and work. They marked his ill temper and took care not to arouse his further anger. In the morning he was up at daybreak and in more gentle mood directed the beginning of the day's labors.

CHAPTER XXII—FAITHFUL AND TRUE

Late that afternoon Arthur and Louise sat in the court, chatting with their guests, who were occupied in coddling and amusing baby Jane, when Inez approached Mr. Weldon and said that Miguel wished to speak with him.

"Send him here," said Arthur, and presently the old Mexican appeared, again arrayed in his best clothes and with the red necktie carefully arranged. He held his hat in his hand and looked uncertainly around the circle. Then his eyes wandered to the nursery and through the open door he saw Mildred sitting in a rocker, engaged in reading a book. Runyon had gone home that morning, "to see if the ranch is still there," he said.

"I have—some—private talks to make, Meest Weld," began the old ranchero.

"Speak out, Miguel," said his master encouragingly.

"Oh; but he said 'private,'" Patsy reminded him.

"I know. Miguel understands that he may speak before my friends."

"It ees—about—Señor Cristoval, Meest Weld."

"Yes? Well, what about him, Miguel?"

"I am once servant for Señor Cristoval. I stay here in house with him, long time. When he get sick, before he die, I care for him. Doctor say to me that Señor Cristoval can not get well; I say so to Señor Cristoval. He say never mind, he have live long enough."

This was interesting to them all in view of the recent happenings, and the girls bent nearer to hear the old man's story. Arthur, the major and Uncle John were equally intent.

"Señor Cristoval, he say, when he get very bad, there ees one thing he hate to leave, an' that ees—his money," continued Miguel. "He say, money

149

ees his bes' friend, all time. But he no can take money where he will go. He ees mad that many poor fools will spend the money he have love an' cared for. So he make me take three big bag of gold an' drive to bank an' put away so the poor fools will find it. Much more money ees in bank, too. Then, when doctor come, he ask me when he will die, an' doctor say when sun next shine Señor Cristoval will not see it. Doctor want to stay all night, but Señor Cristoval pay an' tell him go. He want to die alone.

"But I am there. Some time in night Señor Cristoval he call an' say: 'Miguel, I mus' not die till I have give to Leighton what belong to him. I have keep Leighton's money for him. I will show you where it ees hid, so you can give it to Leighton.'"

Ah, they were intent enough now. Intuitively each listener seemed to know that a secret was about to be revealed and many glances were cast toward the unconscious Mildred, who continued to read placidly. But no one interrupted the old Mexican.

"I help Senor Cristoval to stand up. He ees not strong, so I hold him. He walk from blue room to back room an' there he show me how to take block from wall. Behind block ees big place for money. Señor Cristoval he say all money what belong to Leighton ees there. He tell me count it. So I put Señor Cristoval in chair an' he watch while I take out money an' count. There ees four bag. I count three bag an' he say good, it ees right. He say count last bag. So I empty bag on floor an' count gold an' put in bag again. When thees ees done I say: 'Is eet right?' But Señor Cristoval say nothing. I look up, an' Señor Cristoval ees dead."

The old man spoke simply and quietly, but they found his relation intensely dramatic. Patsy was trembling with excitement. Beth clasped Louise's hand and found it cold from nervousness.

"And then, Miguel?" said Arthur.

"Then, Meest Weld, I put gold in wall an' fix block so no one know an' carry Señor Cristoval to his bed. That ees all, Meest Weld."

"And you told no one of Leighton's gold?"

"I tell no one. It ees belong to Leighton."

"Where is it now, Miguel?"

"In wall, Meest Weld."

"All of it?"

"All."

There was a moment's pause.

"You know now that it belongs to Mildred—to Leighton's daughter,—do you not?" he asked, an accent of sternness in his voice.

"I know, Meest Weld."

"Then why did you not tell us of this before?"

Old Miguel stood silent, shifting from one foot to another, his eyes cast down, his slender brown fingers spasmodically pressing the rim of his sombrero. But when he spoke it was in his former quiet manner.

"I am a bad man, Meest Weld. I theenk I keep gold for myself. Why not, when no one know? Long time after Señor Cristoval die no one come here. Some time I go to room an' count gold. When I see it I have bad thought. I theenk it ees nice if I keep all myself. But when I go away an' work in the grove, I tell Miguel many time that gold ees not his; it ees Leighton's gold. I say when Leighton come for it he mus' have it. But Leighton do not come. Many year the gold ees mine, an' no one know. Then come Leighton's girl, an' I know I am bad man if I keep gold. But I say nothing. I theenk no one ever know."

"But tell me," said Arthur curiously, "what good is the money to you when it is hidden in a wall?"

"Not much, Meest Weld; but I know I am rich. I say I can buy ranch an' be big man, an' no one know I have steal Leighton's gold."

"Then why have you told us the secret?"

Miguel glanced toward the nursery.

"I am man for work," said he. "Always I work; always I mus' work. I am old. When I can no work, I mus' die. Señor Cristoval mus' leave gold when he die; it ees same with Miguel. Now I have good job. I can work an' be happy. But—"

"Well, Miguel?"

"Leighton's daughter, she ees a girl. A girl can not work like a man. It ees her gold, not mine. When you say it, I will show you where Leighton's gold ees hid."

Uncle John sprang up and grasped the man's hand.

"You are an honest fellow, Miguel!" he cried.

"No, Meest Mereek," was the reply. "I have wish to steal, so I am not honest."

"But you have given up the gold."

"Yes, Meest Mereek; because I am afraid."

"I don't believe a word of it," said Patsy. "You were tempted to do wrong, Miguel, and if you had kept silent no one would ever have known; but you told us of the gold, and so you are faithful and true."

"Ah, that ees what Meest Leighton tell me, some time," said he. "An' that ees what spoil me from being bad. Because Leighton say I am faithful an' true, I have theenk I mus' be that way. That ees it."

———

Mildred's gold proved to be a small fortune. Perhaps Cristoval had added to his partner's earnings, for the child's sake, for the total amounted to more than she had ever expected.

It was all in hard cash and Arthur drove over to the bank and deposited it to the credit of Mildred Travers, as she preferred to retain that name.

Patsy and Beth were curious to know what the girl would do with her windfall, but Mildred proved noncommittal.

"How about Bul Run?" asked Patsy.

Mildred smiled but blushed deeply at the question.

"Would my money be enough to pay his mortgages?" she inquired.

"Perhaps," said Beth, "but that would be foolish. He would soon be in debt again."

"No, no!" protested Patsy. "I'm sure he will reform if—"

"If Mildred marries him?"

"Yes."

Mildred seemed troubled.

"The best way," declared Beth, "would be to have Mildred keep her money in her own name, and help out in case of emergency."

Mildred approved that, and being pressed by the two girls she frankly confided to them that she would accept Mr. Runyon when he came for his answer.

Runyon appeared on the third day and Arthur met him and told him the good news of the finding of Mildred's inheritance. But the effect of this discovery on the big rancher was to overwhelm him with despair.

"She will never marry me now," he asserted in doleful tones, "and I'd rather die than ask her. It would be beastly to take such an advantage of the poor child. When she was poor, I could offer her a home with good grace, but now that she's rolling in gold the jig is up! If you'll tell me, where I can find old Miguel, I'll strangle the villain. Why in thunder couldn't he hold his tongue?"

Arthur laughingly replied that money wouldn't make a particle of difference with a girl like Mildred, but Runyon would not listen and remained disconsolate. He stayed at the ranch, but moped around with a woe-begone countenance and refused to speak with anyone.

Patsy and Beth skillfully contrived several opportunities for Runyon to approach Mildred, but he ignored all chances and preferred to remain miserable. The day passed without his demanding his answer. Mildred had been bright and expectant and the girls read her disappointment when her unaccountable wooer delayed putting his fortune to the test.

The next day he was no more cheerful, but rather seemed to have accumulated an added gloom. He sought a garden bench and smoked innumerable cigars in solitary grief. If anyone approached, Runyon would retreat to the shrubbery. At mealtime he was likewise silent but consumed enormous quantities of food, which made Patsy accuse him of being an impostor.

"No regulation lover," she said to him, "ever had an appetite. The novels all say so. Therefore you can't love Mildred a bit."

Runyon groaned, cast her a reproachful glance and went on eating.

Several days passed without his asking Mildred for her answer, and now the absurd situation began to get on all their nerves. Mildred herself grew impatient and watched from the nursery window the garden bench on which Runyon sat gloomily in his perpetual cloud of smoke.

"He'll make himself sick, with those black cigars, I'm sure," observed Patsy, on one occasion.

"And he can't afford to smoke so many," added Beth. "Unless this thing stops, he'll soon have to take out a new mortgage."

"Or sell some lemons," added Patsy.

"I believe," said Mildred slowly, as if summoning her courage, "I will speak to him myself. Don't you think that would be best?"

"Of course," approved Patsy. "Runyon is a big baby, and needs a nurse more than little Jane. I'll hold Toodlums, Mildred, while you sally forth and take the bull by the horns."

Mildred looked at Beth for counsel.

"Unless you speak to him," said that young lady, "you will never get together. Moreover, the rest of us will grow mad or idiotic. So, for all our sakes, you'd better take Mr. Runyon in hand. You'll have to manage him afterward, anyhow, so the sooner you begin the better."

Mildred handed little Jane to Patsy and left the nursery. Through the window the other girls watched her approach Mr. Runyon and stand before him. At once he stood up and threw away his cigar, but his face was toward them and they could see that he did not speak.

Mildred, however, was talking very earnestly. Runyon shook his head. He turned half away. Then he swung sharply around and caught the girl in his arms.

"Come, Beth," said Patsy; "let's go and tell Louise."